THE PUZZLE
OF PIRI REIS

A Tony Boudreaux Mystery

The *Tony Boudreaux Mystery* Series:

The Crystal Skull Murders
Death in the French Quarter
The Swamps of Bayou Teche
Extracurricular Murder
The Ying on Triad
Death in the Distillery
Skeletons of the Atchafalaya
Galveston
Vicksburg

Other Mysteries by Kent Conwell:

The Riddle of Mystery Inn

THE PUZZLE
OF PIRI REIS

•

Kent Conwell

AVALON BOOKS
NEW YORK

Published by Thomas Bouregy & Co., Inc.
160 Madison Avenue, New York, NY 10016

Library of Congress Cataloging-in-Publication Data

Conwell, Kent.
The puzzle of Piri Reis / Kent Conwell.
    p. cm. — (The Tony Boudreaux mystery series)
    ISBN 978-0-8034-9958-4
1. Private investigators—Texas—Austin—Fiction.   I. Title.

PS3553.0547P88 2009
813'.54—dc22   2008052529

PRINTED IN THE UNITED STATES OF AMERICA
ON ACID-FREE PAPER
BY HADDON CRAFTSMEN, BLOOMSBURG, PENNSYLVANIA

To Susan, who has little time to read now since Mikey
came along a couple years back.
And to my wife, Gayle.

Chapter One

I'd had enough excitement in the last four months to last me four years.

Somehow, I managed to survive the claustrophobic catacombs last summer beneath the St. Louis Cemetery in New Orleans. A couple of months later, a torched hip-hop club on Austin's Sixth Street tossed me head over heels into a web of murder and assassinations involving a crystal skull, a two-million-dollar diamond heist, and a band of Mesoamerican fanatics who killed without remorse.

So naturally, the last thing I now wanted to deal with was Ice Age civilizations, six-thousand-year-old maps, Egyptian hieroglyphics that were not Egyptian hieroglyphics, and the malarkey-filled idea that mankind came from a colony of misfits dumped on Earth by advanced civilizations from outer space.

The kooks were coming out of the woodwork, and I was too exhausted to fool with them. All I wanted to do was stay in Austin for a couple of months, handle a few simple, non-threatening insurance or surveillance gigs, and go home at night and relax.

The most excitement I wanted was dinner dancing with Janice Coffman-Morrison, my off-again, on-again Significant Other, or feeding AB, my little teenaged cat I'd saved from a couple of backwater Neanderthals on Bayou Teche who'd wanted to use him for alligator bait.

Now, I've handled cases that had me going in half a dozen different directions all at the same time, but the crystal skull arson caper was the most confusing.

I didn't figure I could ever run into a case any more bewildering or convoluted, but as usual, I was wrong.

I got my first surprise of the day when I walked into the office a few minutes before eight on Monday. My boss, Marty Blevins, was in his glassed-in office, and with a visitor, a male in a tan suit.

Knowing Marty, I figured money was somehow involved. A creature of habit, he never darkened the office door before nine, and then usually closer to ten. For him to be in at this hour meant money was on the table, a lot of money.

If I'd known two hours earlier what was coming, I would have had no compunction calling in sick, claiming a bad case of water on the knee or shingles on the shin.

When Marty spotted me, he waved me to his office. The hair on the back of my neck tingled.

Marty rose when I entered and gestured to the man in the suit. "Tony, this is Ted Odom. Ted, meet Tony Boudreaux."

Rising and shifting a manila folder from one hand to the other, Odom nodded. "Nice to meet you, Tony." He extended his free hand.

The pasty-faced man's skin was clammy and his grip nonexistent. I guessed him to be in his early to mid-forties and about forty pounds overweight. "Same here, Mr. Odom."

Clearing his throat, Marty continued. "Mr. Odom is from San Antonio."

"That's good," I replied, figuring that was as appropriate a response as any.

Marty turned to Odom. "Tony's the one you were asking about."

My eyes narrowed in suspicion. "Oh?"

Running his fat finger under his unbuttoned collar around his fleshy neck, Marty cleared his throat, and with nonchalant indifference, explained. "Mr. Odom has inherited a valuable map."

I nodded to Odom. "Congratulations." What else could I say?

"Oh, I don't have it, Tony. It's been stolen. At least, I think so. That's why I've come to you. I want you to find it. I heard from a friend about the crystal skull you uncovered a couple months back." He paused, waiting for a response from me.

The crystal skull! The memories it brought back were less than pleasant. I just stared at him.

When I didn't reply, he blinked his watery eyes and continued. "I know something about ancient art, and I am familiar with the stories of the crystal skulls. They are quite valuable." He paused, glanced at Marty, then back to me. "But the Piri Reis Map is ten times more valuable than even the Nelson-Vines Crystal Skull, which, as you know, is not only anatomically correct but also has a removable jawbone." He paused once again and turned to Marty. "From a technical standpoint, Mr. Blevins, not even today's most talented sculptors or engineers could duplicate the Nelson-Vines Crystal Skull, which is purported to be thousands of years old."

Marty frowned at me. He had no idea what the soft-looking little man was talking about. "He's right, Marty," I replied. "About the skull." I seriously considered feigning a heart attack at that moment just to get away from what I knew was coming.

Odom waggled an almost translucent finger in the air. "There is much intrigue about the Piri Reis Map, but that which is most arresting is the fact that the map shows the western coast of Africa, the eastern coast of South America, and the northern coast of Antarctica, which is perfectly detailed before the coming of glaciers. According to core samples from the Ross Sea, the last time that particular area shown in the map was free of ice was more than six thousand years ago."

Marty nodded eagerly, like a puppy anticipating a juicy bone. "You don't say."

I rolled my eyes at his eloquence.

Taking a deep breath and releasing it quickly, Odom chewed on his thin lips. "That's why I'm here, Tony. I want to retain you to find the map." He looked at Marty. "I'm willing to go as high as fifty thousand dollars."

Talk about a juicy bone. Marty's fat jowls flopped wildly as he nodded. Then a shrewd gleam glittered in his eyes. "Our policy is a five-thousand-dollar retainer plus expenses even if we are unable to complete the commission."

Odom nodded emphatically. "Certainly. Make it a ten-thousand-dollar retainer. It's yours even if you don't find the map."

Marty beamed. "If any of my boys can find your map, Mr. Odom, it's Tony." He winked at me. "Right, Tony?"

I didn't know anything about the map, but if Odom compared it to the crystal skulls, then I didn't want any part of it. For a fleeting second, my options ran through my head. I could retire. Lots of people retire before forty. Of course, I needed money. Last time I balanced my checkbook, I had enough to last maybe a year if I ate nothing but Vienna sausage. After that . . . well, maybe I could convince Janice to marry me. After all, she was rich. As a last resort, I could talk Jack Edney, my multi-millionaire pal, into taking me in as a partner managing one of his chains of condo complexes. If those options didn't pan out, I could always join my old man hopping freights and sleeping in alleys.

Or I could take the assignment.

I drew a deep breath. Maybe it wouldn't be so bad. At least looking for a map, nobody gets shot, chopped, maimed, slashed, or killed. With a sappy grin, I shrugged. "Why not? Sounds interesting." Besides, I reminded myself, I'd always liked San Antonio, especially the River Walk, a tropical venue that bisects downtown. Swanky hotels, five-star restaurants, and exotic bars lined the walk's flagstone sidewalks. The city's playground was an adequate second cousin for those of us who couldn't afford some more intriguing locales such as Cancun, St. Martin, Puerto Vallarta, or for the very daring, Turtle Island in Fiji.

Back at my desk, I pulled out a notepad and glanced at Ted Odom in the battered chair across the desk from me. "All right, Mr. Odom. A few details. This map, what did you call it?"

Laying the manila folder on my desk, he pursed his thin lips and stared at the ceiling for several seconds pondering his reply. "Piri Reis. It was discovered at the Imperial Palace in Constantinople in 1929. It was painted on parchment and dated 919 in the Islamic calendar, which translates to 1513 in ours. The map was signed by Piri Ibn Haji Memmed, also known as Piri Reis, an admiral from the Turkish Navy." He paused. "That's why it's called the Piri Reis Map."

I managed not to roll my eyes. "I see."

He nodded. "According to him, the map was put together from a set of twenty or so maps drawn in the time of Alexander the Great."

Alexander the Great! All I knew about him was he conquered everybody in the world around three or four hundred years BC. I couldn't help thinking that if someone had drawn that map from other maps during his time, the chart had to be almost as old as dirt. "Piri Reis," I replied, jotting down the name.

"Yes. P-I-R-I R-E-I-S. Piri Reis."

"You inherited the map, you say?"

His brows knit. "Unfortunately. You see, someone murdered my father and stole the map."

It felt like a sledgehammer hit me between the eyes. I had just come out of a tangle of murders and I didn't need any more. I blinked once or twice, hoping I'd misunderstood the slight man. "Murdered?"

Taking a deep breath, he released it slowly. "Well, the police think my father just fell and hit his head. They found him on the floor in his den where he conducted his business."

"But you don't think so."

He shook his head. "I have no proof except that Father always sensed he might be murdered for the map. He was paranoid about it, and now the map is missing. I guess the old man was right. I just put two and two together and came up with four."

I groaned to myself. Another two-and-two-is-four weirdo. "Why didn't you go to the police? Let them handle it."

"I did. My cousin, Louis, is chief of police. He refused. Said the JP ruled it an accidental death."

"A JP? Not a medical examiner?"

He looked at me curiously. "No. George Elkins. He's our Justice of the Peace. He's been re-elected for the last twenty years."

I started to make a sarcastic remark but bit my tongue. "What did the autopsy show?"

He shook his head. "There wasn't one."

I muttered a curse to myself. I'd been in the business long enough to learn that half the time JPs issue incorrect verdicts, but in their little communities their word is as good as a big-city forensic scientist. "Oh," was all I said.

Odom added, "Besides, there's always the publicity. If someone did steal the map, too much publicity might frighten them into destroying it. I can't take that chance."

As much as I hated to admit it, I could understand his concern. "So, the map is missing. You think someone stole it."

A perplexed frown knit his pale forehead. "Well, I don't know for sure."

Now, he really had me confused. I had the unsettling feeling I had stepped into a time warp and was the center of a comic routine in a silent film. "I don't understand. You said the map was missing. Someone must have taken it."

Beads of perspiration popped out on his face. "Let

me explain. My father was not the kind of man to stumble over an ottoman like the police surmised. He was sixty-seven, walked regularly, climbed stairs. He was quite agile." He paused and lowered his gaze to his white hands. "I might be wrong, but I have a gut feeling about it. Someone wanted the map, and when Father refused, they killed him."

Leaning back in my chair, I glanced through the glass walls at Marty, who had his head bowed, intently studying something on his desk. "Did you mention this to Mr. Blevins? I mean, about your father."

"Oh, yes," he replied ingenuously, his dark eyes smiling. "He said since the police ruled the death was accidental, his agency could handle the case."

Marty was right. Still, I preferred jobs where I had no dealings whatsoever with dead people. "Mr. Odom, I don't know if Mr. Blevins explained it or not but we have to be certain there is no ongoing police investigation. Otherwise we will not involve ourselves."

For a moment, a flash of anger erased the glittering smile in his eyes but quickly vanished. "Certainly. And," he added with a hint of smugness, "all of that is taken care of. I made sure of that before I drove up here."

With a cynical frown, I replied, "Oh? And just how did you pull off that little miracle?"

"I told you. My cousin, Louis Ibbara—the police chief."

My frown deepened. "Of the San Antonio force?"

"The San Madreas police force, where we live. When

San Antonio took us in over forty years ago, we kept our own civil and judicial infrastructure." He paused and added, "And Louis said since they do not have a criminal investigation going, you're more than welcome to our little community."

Chapter Two

I shot Marty another hard look. This time he was staring in my direction, but as soon as my eyes met his, he looked away. I drew a deep breath. "All right, Mr. Odom. I'm—"

"Please, Tony, call me Ted."

I shivered. "All right, Ted. Like I started to say, I'm puzzled here. This map. You can't find it. Right?"

Resting an elbow on the desk, he leaned forward. "Yes. You see, my father was Bernard Julius Odom, BJ Odom." He paused and looked at me expectantly as if the name should mean something to me.

I lifted my eyebrows. "So?"

His brows knit in surprise. "The puzzle king?"

I shook my head slowly. "Nope. Sorry."

He looked at me in disbelief, then lifted an eyebrow and said, "He was one of the most widely recognized

11

puzzle writers in the country. Crosswords, double acrostics, secret shape word searches, codes and ciphers. His puzzles have been published in national newspapers and magazines for almost forty-five years."

That spiel meant nothing to me. I hate puzzles, any kind of puzzle. I'd rather argue with my ex-wife than attempt a puzzle. "What does that have to do with the map?"

He stared at me a moment, then shook his head. "Nothing really. I just thought you might like to know about him. He was an important man."

I suppressed the urge to reply with a whoop-de-do. I smiled reassuringly. "I'm sure he was. Now, the map? Why do you believe it's missing?"

"Over the years, any number of individuals have wanted the map. And in fairness to them, they all offered fair prices. Just after acquiring the map about five years ago, Father hid it."

Now, the guy was beginning to make a little sense. "And he didn't tell anyone where he hid it?"

"No. I thought he might mention its location in his will, but he didn't."

I frowned. "Kind of thoughtless, huh?"

Ted missed my subtle zinger. Seriously, he replied, "Father was like that. He was, well, different." He held up his hands to the heavens in frustration. "Anyway, I searched his office and even his safety deposit boxes although I knew it wouldn't be there. In the safety deposit boxes, I mean."

"Oh? And why is that?"

"Why, he always said so." When he saw the frown on my face, he continued. "Father always told me the location of the map was in his den but I searched every inch of the den. Nothing. Besides, the map is on parchment, and none of Father's safety deposit boxes were large enough for the map."

"Just how large is it?"

He held his hands several inches apart. "Forty-five-by-sixty-one centimeters." From the box he was making with his hands, I figured the map was about eighteen by twenty-four inches. He picked up the folder from the desk and handed it to me. "Here. This is the history of the map, which has been studied by various universities and military commissions."

The folder contained a half-inch-thick sheath of single-spaced pages. I whistled softly.

He laughed. "When do you think you can start, Tony?"

I glanced at my uncluttererd desktop, then at Marty. "Give me a day or two to clear my desk."

"Is there anything you need me to do in preparation?"

I hesitated. "You said there were several who offered to buy the map. Do you think any of them would be capable of stealing the map or, as you think, murdering him?"

He shook his head emphatically. "No. Oh, some didn't care for Father. He was sort of arrogant. He wasn't an easy man to like, but I can't believe any of them capable of his death, nor can I believe any of them would steal the map."

I listened to him with a jaundiced mind. I'd seen too many seemingly honorable individuals turn out to possess the morals and integrity of a feral cat. "Well, maybe not. Anyway, make me a list of them. When I get there, we'll look around the den and see what we can come up with." I paused. "See if we can find a starting spot."

Watching Ted Odom leave, I wondered if he were capable of his father's murder. He appeared to have been indulged most of his life. He was soft and artless.

From the corner of my eye, a figure appeared. I looked up. It was Marty. With the innocence of a child, he asked, "Well, what do you think?"

"Why didn't you tell me the old man might have been murdered?"

His eyes grew wide in surprise. "No need. The police said it was an accident. There is no investigation for us to worry about."

Of course, Marty was right, but I couldn't help wondering just how certain the San Madreas JP was that Odom's death was an accident. From what I knew of JPs, some of their decisions were crapshoots. "What if it turns out his death wasn't an accident?"

Marty shrugged. "We back away, and keep the ten Gs." A leering grin plastered his pan-shaped face. He laughed and slapped me on the shoulder. "You worry too much, Tony. Just get down there and find the map.

Think about it. Your share of fifty thousand is five big ones, right?"

Marty always could find a way to be persuasive.

After work, I rushed home, fed AB, then plopped down on the couch with a cold Old Milwaukee beer to peruse the folder Ted Odom had given me.

I had about an hour or so to spare before I picked up Janice for our eight o'clock dinner date. As usual, we would, as she so primly phrased it, *dine* at the Commodore Plaza Hotel overlooking the Colorado River at the Congress Street Bridge in downtown Austin.

The date was an impromptu surprise, for she had called me the day before and suggested in her inimitable rich girl's way that she wouldn't mind dinner and dancing at the Commodore Plaza. Such a spontaneous call was unusual for her. For the most part, she was a purposeful young lady, and for her, one day's notice was impulsive. I had a feeling she had something on her mind other than dinner and dancing.

Naturally, I suggested the next night at eight. And naturally, she accepted. Janice was used to getting her way.

She and I met a few years back when I helped her out of an insurance jam. She was the only heir to one of the largest distilleries in Texas. Neither she nor I was interested in getting serious, but we had fun together even though I quickly realized I was simply a dependable escort, an infrequent lover, an occasional confidant.

In other words, I was a tool to satisfy her various needs. And she was the same for me. We had reconciled our positions in our relationship. And both were fairly content with the status quo.

Inexplicably, despite our skewed relationship, from time to time Janice did speak of *our relationship*. After a few of those little discussions, which I really didn't understand, I learned when to agree and when not to agree.

Once, she had even worked a case with me, but the thrill and challenge of long hours, unpleasant surroundings, and even more, unpleasant individuals, could not in any way compare to the tedium of a gambling jaunt to Monte Carlo or a boring weeklong ski trip to Vail.

She gave up investigative work, but in fairness to her, she did a gutsy job on that case with me, just as gutsy a job as any tough woman could turn out.

Reading through the folder of material, I could only shake my head in disbelief at such nonsense. That the Piri Reis Map actually existed was evident, but much of the background and theories linked with the map stretched belief beyond the breaking point.

There was no way I could believe navigators had mapped the shoreline of Antarctica thousands of years before it froze over, or that in 9500 BC, because of a polar shift, the continent had moved hundreds of miles from the north to its present position.

And there was no way I could choke down the theory that the detailed accuracy of the map was the result of aerial mapping six thousand years ago. After reading that off-the-wall hypothesis, I tossed aside the folder in disgust.

Oh, yes, there was one other thing that boggled my mind. I couldn't believe there were imbeciles out there willing to spend thousands of dollars on such garbage. On the other hand, I once again reminded myself that somewhere out there is always one more imbecile than you expected.

At that moment, AB hopped up on the couch and curled up beside me. I grinned and scratched him behind the ears. "A bunch of nonsense, little guy," I muttered. "Makes you wonder what woodwork these guys come out of, huh?"

AB just purred contentedly, and despite my AA vows, I popped open a second beer.

As usual, Janice was a knockout.

Having grown up in Church Point, Louisiana, on my grandfather's farm until Mom moved us to Austin when I started high school, I figured everyone was just like us.

I discovered my mistake when I met Janice. Everyone was not like us. Other than the normal human appendages, the only thing the very rich have in common with the rest of us is nothing. Their speech is different; they carry themselves differently; their tastes are unique; even their attitudes are distinctive.

Janice never shopped at Wal-Mart or Penney's. I don't think she even knew that such merchants existed.

Her clothes, whether simple or elaborate, screamed *haute couture*, obscenely expensive.

That night was no exception. She wore a simple white sheath dress with long sleeves and lacy cuffs about her wrists and an identical collar caressing her slender neck. Her diamond earrings and necklace sparkled like a ten-foot Christmas tree. And even if you screwed up the nerve to ask, she couldn't tell you what they cost. Her typical response was, "No idea. I bought them because I liked them."

The maitre d' saw us enter and hurried to escort Janice to her favorite table by the windows overlooking the river. I ordered white chardonnay, her favorite. For dinner, she ordered *terrine de saumon aux epinards—riz spécial*, salmon and spinach terrine with rice. I never cared for the classic French cuisine, primarily because the traditional French in which the menus were printed was nothing like the Cajun French patois with which I grew up in Church Point. Consequently, I learned one entrée and side dish that I ordered every time we dined French, *filet mignon aux oignons—gratin dauphinois,* pork filet mignon with onions and a baked potato.

As the waiter left, Janice rested her elbows on the table, folded her hands together, and laid her chin on her slender fingers. She smiled warmly. "I'm glad you could make it tonight, Tony. I've missed you."

Her remarks puzzled me. We'd been out the previous Friday, three days earlier. "I missed you too." I started to ask her what was on her mind but instead I rose and offered my hand. "Dance?"

We danced until our dinner was served.

As I held her chair for her, I leaned forward and whispered in her ear. "Are you all right?"

She frowned up at me. "Yes. Why do you ask?"

I shrugged as I sat across the table from her. "I don't know. You seem different tonight."

Her eyes lit despite a tiny frown wrinkling her forehead. "Different? Oh, and how is that?" She made an effort to be coy.

Smiling, I laid my hand on hers. "I can't put my finger on it but you seem different tonight. You're always radiant but tonight you seem even more so."

She squeezed my hand. "That's because I've been thinking about us, Tony."

I chuckled. "Good things, I hope."

"Oh, yes." She beamed and squeezed my hand again. "Tony, I've been thinking about you and thought that maybe it's time for us to talk about getting married."

Chapter Three

My life flashed before my eyes. I was at a loss for words. We had joked about marriage in the past, but nothing serious. I gave her a weak grin. "Okay. I'll bite. What's the punchline?"

Her brows knit and her smile faded. Then, figuring I was just pulling her leg, which I might add, was a very attractive leg to pull, she laughed. "Now, stop clowning around, Tony. I'm serious. We've been together for a few years, and maybe we should think about moving on with our lives."

My *Grand-père* Moise always cautioned me never to believe that I knew how a woman really felt. Only God knew, and at times, even though He created her, He was mistaken. Despite that warning, I couldn't believe Janice was serious. Not wanting to offend her, I tentatively replied, "Well, you're right about moving on. I haven't really thought about it that much, but then you know, whenever the subject has come up in the past we've always joked about it."

She smiled knowingly. "That was then."

Searching for the right words, I grabbed my glass of chardonnay and with trembling hand, very delicately chugged down the remainder. "Have—have you talked to your Aunt Beatrice about it?" Beatrice Morrison was the CEO of Chalk Hills Distillery, the largest distillery in Texas. Head of Austin society, she carried herself with the regal disdain of a modern-day Cleopatra. After Janice's parents died, Beatrice adopted her. Janice was Beatrice's only living relative, and one day Janice would be worth more than the Queen of England.

Her smile grew sad. "No. Aunt Beatrice hasn't been well. I—I didn't want to excite her until I knew how you felt."

I sensed a degree of reluctance on her part. Leaning across the table, I laid my hand on hers. She looked into my eyes, and I made sure to pick my words carefully. "It would be a big step, Janice, especially for you. You know how I feel. You and me, we're, well, we come from different backgrounds. You—"

At that moment, her cell phone rang. She ignored it. It rang again. "Isn't that your cell?"

She nodded. "Whoever it is will leave a message."

I wasn't as concerned about the message as much as I was a golden opportunity to sidetrack the direction of our conversation. "It might be important."

With a sigh, she fished the little phone from her

diamond-encrusted purse and answered. She stared at me, her eyes growing wide in alarm. "Which hospital?" She nodded. "Fine. I'll meet you there." She punched off and stared at me in disbelief. "It's Aunt Beatrice. She's had a heart attack."

At 2:00 A.M., Beatrice's doctor informed us it was angina instead of a heart attack. Still, they wanted to keep her overnight.

I nodded and squeezed Janice's hand. "I'll take you home."

She pulled away. "No. I'll spend the night here."

"Okay. I'll stay with you."

She shook her head. "That's sweet of you but it isn't necessary. Aunt Beatrice has a private room with two beds. Besides, one of the maids will be here if we need anything."

I studied her a moment, admiring the cool aplomb with which she faced the situation. "All right. You have my cell number. I've got a job down in San Antonio. I'm leaving in the morning. I'll call before I go."

Standing on her tiptoes, she smiled sweetly and touched her delicate lips to mine. "Thank you, Tony."

During the drive back to my apartment, my head reeled with confusion. While I don't possess the inherent intuitiveness of Al Grogan, the top investigator in our agency, the years working with him had begun to hone the PI mentality in me. I tried to analyze just

what had happened that night. Her suggestion of marriage had come out of nowhere. Why? What prompted
it? Could it be she was serious? Did she truly want to
marry me? I couldn't believe her aunt agreed with her
choice of mates.

Beatrice tolerated me, pure and simple.

Flexing my fingers about the steering wheel, I muttered softly, "After all, Tony, she's rich, and you do
care for her." I came up with half a dozen other reasons to marry Janice, but for some reason the prospect
just didn't appeal to me. Was it simply a matter of cold
feet? Or the fact I just didn't want to marry again after
one bad marriage?

At 2:50, I pulled into my drive. It had been a long
day, and tomorrow would be even longer.

Before I left next morning, I made reservations at the
Grand Isle Inn on the River Walk in San Antonio, then
called the hospital. Beatrice was doing well. "She had a
good night. Call me when you settle in," Janice said.
"I'm staying with Aunt Beatrice until she's released."

"Right."

To my relief, she didn't mention our conversation
from the night before, and I certainly didn't.

When Mom had moved us to Austin twenty-odd
years earlier, the ninety or so mile drive from Austin to
San Antonio had been broken only by a mere handful of
small hill-country towns. Today, just about every single

mile is filled with malls, service stations, curio shops, discount centers, car lots, and any of a thousand other businesses catering to the public.

Twenty-odd years ago, most of the traffic, other than eighteen-wheelers, had been University of Texas students visiting the open arms of exotic entertainment in San Antonio or farther south at Nuevo Laredo. Today, all lanes, both north and south, were jammed with bumper-to-bumper traffic, and exotic entertainment could be enjoyed at the top and bottom of every hill.

I hit the interstate just before nine after stopping off at the police station and convincing Chief Pachuca to put in a good word for me with the police chief at San Madreas, Louis Ibbara.

He eyed me suspiciously. "Why?"

I explained I was only trying to find a missing map. He agreed.

Chief Pachuca and I went back a few years. I always made a point of never sticking my nose in his business nor stepping over the lines he drew for me. Two or three times, my nosing around helped him, and he always remembered.

So, tooling along I-35 that morning at sixty-five in my Chevrolet Silverado pickup, the only thing I had on my mind was Janice's suggestion of marriage from the night before and why she had not mentioned it in our conversation that morning. Then the thought hit me that maybe she hadn't mentioned it for the same reason I hadn't. Or maybe she was simply worried about her aunt.

I passed a black eighteen-wheel Peterbilt tractor and a red Dodge Ram pickup. I couldn't help noticing the big tractor had a dealer's license taped to the back window. Half a mile ahead, I spotted the bridge spanning the San Marcos River. I pulled back into the right lane. Moments later, from the corner of my eye, an object loomed on my left, filling the window. I glanced over and to my stunned horror, spotted a massive black tire as big as my pickup only inches from my truck. The huge, eighteen-wheel tractor I had just passed had pulled up beside me and was easing into my lane, forcing me onto the shoulder.

I laid down on the Klaxon horn but he ignored me.

Suddenly, steel guardrails loomed ahead. Muttering a curse though my clenched teeth, I slammed on the brakes, released them, touched them again, stomped on the emergency brake and spun the wheel to the right, hoping the weeklong driving class Marty had sent me to a few years earlier would pay off.

To my relief, the pickup did a one-eighty and slid onto the grass beyond the graveled shoulder, only inches from the guardrails. Woodenly, I dropped the transmission into park and sagged back on the seat, my heart thudding against my chest like a bass drum pounded by a deranged drummer down on Sixth Street. I closed my eyes.

Moments later, I heard a tapping on the window. I opened my eyes to see a burr-headed young man staring at me in alarm.

"You all right, mister?"

Slowly, I rolled down the window and nodded. "Yeah. Yeah. A little shook up, but I'm okay."

He shot a withering look at the highway. "That idiot almost ran me off the road trying to get to you."

I blinked once or twice. "What's that?"

Nodding emphatically, he said, "Yeah. He'd been following me for several miles. After you passed us, he pulled out and came after you. What'd you do to the guy?"

"Do? Nothing."

The young man arched an eyebrow. "Well, I don't know for certain, but like I said, it sure looked like that joker was deliberately trying to run you off the road. I tried to get a license number, but he didn't have no plates."

After the young man left, I waited another few minutes to still my shaking hands before pulling back on the road. I always expected some drivers to be rude or thoughtless, and more than once they've inadvertently forced me into another lane or to slam on my brakes. Other than cursing their ancestry, I forgot about them.

This one? Well, I didn't know.

After a few miles, I pushed the incident from my mind. The driver probably had no idea he had run me off the road. I figured the young man was just letting his imagination run away with him.

San Madreas is a subdivision of San Antonio, having been absorbed by the burgeoning city decades earlier.

One of the stipulations before the community accepted San Antonio's offer to annex was that the community could keep its own civil and judicial infrastructure. I couldn't help thinking it was sort of like Mayberry in the middle of San Antonio.

The San Madreas police, if Chief Louis Ibbara was any indication, were very informal. Casual and laid-back were also apt descriptions. I was shown to a briefing room at the rear of the station where three officers were bent over their desks in one corner completing their shift reports. In another corner, a lanky, middle-aged man in wrinkled khakis was slumped on a couch drinking a Dr Pepper in front of a blaring TV. His mustache and wavy hair were neatly trimmed and black as night.

Before I had a chance to plead my case, he rose and extended his hand. "You're Boudreaux?"

"Yeah."

He gestured to a refrigerator. "Grab a Coke and have a seat."

While I did as he suggested, he announced, "Ramon Pachuca called me this morning. He said you were okay." He paused and his black eyes grew hard. "Teddy said you were looking for the map."

I nodded and sipped my Coke.

"We're a small community here, Boudreaux. You look for the map and we'll get along fine. Anything I can do to help, let me know."

The warning in his tone was obvious. "No problem."

He grinned. "How was the drive down?"

"Lot of traffic," I replied, saying nothing of the eighteen-wheeler.

"So that skinflint uncle of mine hid the map, huh?"

"Hid? Ted said it was missing. He thought it might be stolen."

Ibbara snorted and gulped a couple of swallows of Dr Pepper. "Teddy's always been an alarmist." He grinned. "It wouldn't surprise me if Uncle Bernard hid it so it would never be found."

His remarked puzzled me. "Why is that?"

His grin faded. "He was hard to get along with. Contrary as sin." He shook his head, his brow knit. "I hate to say it about family but he was a mean man. Selfish. Thought of nobody but himself. Always figured he knew better than everyone, and it galled him when anyone got more attention."

I was confused. "What does that have to do with the map?"

He considered his answer a moment. "That map was his lifetime achievement, something no one else could ever match." He paused and squinted at me. "That make sense?"

"Yeah. That makes sense." I sipped my soft drink. "Ted said his father fell and hit his head."

Ibbara nodded and fished a pack of Marlboros from his shirt pocket. He shook one out and offered it to me but I declined. "Yep. October second. Uncle Bernard was always a preoccupied sort. Looked like he was reading one of those history books of his and wasn't watching where he was walking. Stumbled over an ottoman and hit his forehead on the end table by the couch. When he bounced off, he hit the back of his head on the coffee table. Teddy found him on the floor around eleven."

I grimaced. "Freakish, huh?"

Chief Ibbara screwed up his face in a frown. "Yep. Old George—he's our Justice of the Peace—well, old George said there was no evidence of foul play. He concluded Uncle Bernard tripped and hit his head. A blunt trauma sort of thing, forehead and back of head."

Before I could catch myself, I asked, "Ted said there was no autopsy."

For a moment Ibbara eyed me suspiciously, but the grin on my face told him the question was casual, not probing. "No reason. Uncle Bernard's skull was caved in. Anyone could see that and blood was on the coffee table and end table."

I grimaced. "Freakish, all right. You have any ideas about the map?"

He looked at me like I was crazy. "Me? Nope, not a single one. Uncle Bernard was involved with one of those societies of weirdoes, all caught up in missing continents, aliens from outer space, all that nonsense. Me, I never saw the map. For all I know it might not exist."

I chuckled. "Ted had better hope it does. Otherwise, he's putting up a pretty penny for a lot of nothing."

Chapter Four

Just before two that afternoon, I pulled up at the curb in front of a three-story mansion of white limestone at 2112 Fairchild on a hill overlooking San Madreas and San Antonio. I whistled as I studied the imposing structure. The two diagonal corners of the mansion were cylindrical watchtowers with copper cone-shaped roofs covered with a sheen of green tarnish. A balcony with ornate railings stretched over the front entrance, which could only be reached by puffing your way up a flight of twenty concrete steps. A concrete ramp, wide enough for delivery trucks, led up to the rear entrance, all of which was also covered by a balcony. Spreading oaks dotted the grounds, which took up an entire city block. A spiked wrought-iron fence enclosed the entire grounds.

After managing all twenty of the front steps, I knocked on the door. Moments later it opened, and a slender woman with a waspish face and gray hair pulled into a severe bun stared indifferently at me. She wore a simple one-piece dark blue print dress with a buttoned torso and a thin white belt. "Yes?"

I forced a smile and introduced myself. "I'm here to see Ted Odom."

Recognition flashed in her eyes and her tightly pursed lips blossomed into a thin smile. "Mr. Boudreaux. I've been expecting you." She stepped back, opening the door. "Please, come in. I'm Edna Hudson. I am—I mean, I was—Mr. Odom's private secretary for over thirty years."

She led me to an office in one corner of the house. The interior of the mansion suggested late-nineteenth- or early twentieth-century construction. The wood floors glittered like glass, and upon closer inspection, I saw they were of heart pine wood. A spiral staircase led to the floors above.

As elaborate, as ornate as the house was, it was just as spooky.

In her office, she gestured to a chair as she slipped behind her desk. Resting her left hand in her lap, she smiled primly at me while picking up the phone and punching in the numbers. I glanced around the office, noting the computer hutch behind her desk and the framed snapshots filling the wall around it. A multi-function, all-in-one office machine sat on one end of the hutch.

She replaced the receiver. "Ted'll be right down, Mr. Boudreaux."

I arched an eyebrow. "Oh? He lives here?"

She nodded briskly. "Yes. He has a nice room on the third floor."

Room? On the third floor? A man in his forties? Mentally, I whistled a tune of amazement. "I see. So Ted isn't married?"

"No. He's too young really. He's only thirty-two."

For the second time in as many seconds, I was taken aback. Thirty-two. And I figured him to be in his mid-forties. My estimation of Ted Odom began to change. I've seen forty-five-year-olds look like thirty-two, but the only thirty-two-year-olds I knew who looked forty-five enjoyed lives of absolute dissipation and unqualified indulgence. I tried to hide my confusion. "I see. Does—I mean, did he work with his father or have a business of his own?"

Before Edna could reply, Ted strode in, dressed in gray slacks and a white Polo shirt. "Ah, Tony. Good to see you." He extended his hand. "I see you've met Edna. She's invaluable. Neither Father nor I could get along without her."

I nodded perfunctorily. "I met with Chief Ibbara. I dropped in to pick up the list of names, and take a look at your father's den. Then I'll check in at the hotel."

His eyes widened. He plopped in a red leather wingback chair at the end of Edna's desk. "You can stay here if you wish. There's plenty of room."

The last thing I wanted to do was spend a night in that house. For all I knew, the Frankenstein monster could be hiding behind one of the doors. "No, thanks. Sometimes the job calls for odd hours. I wouldn't want to disturb anyone."

"Oh, you wouldn't be disturbing anyone. After Edna leaves, I'm the only one around."

He just handed me another reason not to stay. Before I could reply, Edna spoke. "Don't nag Mr. Boudreaux, Teddy. He knows his job. He knows what he's doing."

I could have kissed her

Ted shrugged. "Well, whatever. So, now what?"

"The list?"

"Oh, yes." He fished a folded sheet from his pocket and handed it to me. "Here."

I opened the sheet of paper. "Let's see. Ervin Maddox." I glanced at Ted from under my eyebrows.

"He owns an antique shop down on the River Walk. Cassandra's Baubles." He nodded to the list. "The next on the list, Leo Cobb—well, I guess you could call him an art broker."

Edna glanced at her watch on her right wrist. "By the way, Teddy, Mr. Cobb called a couple of hours ago. He wanted to come by and talk to you.'

"Anything important?"

"He didn't say. I told him you were out."

"Did he say what he wanted?"

"No, but I did tell him about the map, and that you were hiring a private investigator to find it. I hope that was all right." She looked at me, then hopefully at Ted.

"He'll find out anyway," he replied. "Don't worry about it, Edna."

She smiled gratefully.

Ted turned to me. "Leo finds artifacts and acts as a middleman between buyer and seller. He and my father were once good friends but they had a falling out."

"Oh." I lifted an eyebrow. "About what?"

"Nothing really. Leo insisted the map was as much his as Father's. They argued about it. Leo swore he would get the map one way or another."

"Why did he think the map was his?"

Pursing his thin lips, Ted hesitated a moment. "As I understand it, he found the map. He claimed Father, as a commission for finding the map, was going to share ownership with him." He shrugged. "Father, of course, denied the allegation."

Tucking that little tidbit of information back in my head, I glanced at the next name. "What about Joe Hogg?"

"He's a rich used-car salesman."

"An unbearable, disgusting man," Edna said bitterly.

Ted laughed. "As you can see, Edna doesn't think much of Joe Hogg."

"Okay, and next, Father Bertoldo Poggioreale." I looked at him in surprise. "Father Bertoldo Poggioreale?"

Ted nodded. "Yes. He's a teacher at L'Università di Grazia e la Fratellanza. He is an expert on ancient maps. In fact, he was a student under the seismologist Reverend William Chanlin, whom the United States Naval Hydrographic Office took to the Antarctic to learn if there was land under the ice as the Piri Reis Map suggested." He paused and glanced at Edna. "Edna can tell you that Father Poggioreale tried, on more than one occasion, to purchase the map from Father."

She nodded. "He did, Mr. Boudreaux. Three times as I remember. Once he even offered two million dollars."

I whistled. "Why does a teacher need a map like this? And where did he get the money?"

Ted shook his head. "I have no idea."

I pulled out my note cards on which I jot all my thoughts and findings. "All right. With you two helping, let's take each name, and you tell me why you think they wanted the map."

Fifteen minutes later, we had finished the job. "Now," I said, pulling out another card, "in addition to these four, who else could have benefited from the map?" I nodded to Ted. "You could, right? You inherited it."

His eyes widened in surprise. "You don't think that I—"

"No. Not at all," I hastened to assure him. "But are there any others?"

He thought a moment. "Only one, I guess. My cousin, Lamia. Lamia Sue Odom. Father took her in when her parents died about fifteen years ago."

Jotting down her name, I nodded. "I see. Was she going to inherit anything?" I looked up from my note cards in time to see a furtive glance pass between Ted and Edna.

"Yes. Father bought a five hundred thousand dollar insurance policy with Lamia as a beneficiary."

I whistled softly.

"He bought one for me also."

"For five hundred thousand?"

With casual nonchalance, he replied, "Yes. Plus the map."

I glanced at Edna who nodded perfunctorily. Good thing it was an accident, I told myself. Otherwise, these two would have dandy motives. "That seems, ah, unusual."

Edna spoke up. "You'd had to have known Mr. Odom. He was fairly eccentric."

Ted chuckled. "Fairly isn't the right word, Edna. Fanatical would be better."

She lowered her gaze to her hands folded in her lap. "I was trying to be nice, Teddy."

Sheepishly, Ted grinned at me. "What she means, Tony, is that Father was a wealthy man. He was worth probably two million or so, not counting the map. He had planned for years to leave the Wingate Museum of Art fifty percent of his estate, Edna fifteen percent, and the remaining thirty-five in trust for maintenance of the estate in perpetuity."

He saw the amazement on my face and quickly explained. "Edna had been with my father for thirty-four years."

"This was my only job," she put in. "Mr. Odom hired me right out of high school. I've been here ever since as his personal secretary." For a moment, I sensed a hint of wistfulness about her.

My fingers were cramping from the notes I was scribbling on the cards. With a relieved sigh, I emphatically popped a period at the end of the sentence and looked up. "What about his niece, Lamia? Does she live here?"

With a wry twist of his lips, Ted glanced upstairs. "Here, in the house? Not quite. She has an apartment in the Elena Towers on the River Walk when she's in town." When I frowned, he explained. "Lamia is one of those free spirits who goes wherever the impulse leads her. She's spent most of her life in Europe. She's been back this time for about six months."

"This time?"

"Yes. She comes back for a few months each year."

I finished taking my notes and slipped the cards back in my pocket.

Ted leaned forward. "So, what's next?"

I studied them a moment. "What about his den?"

"Fine, but first, let me give you a tour of the house. We're quite proud of it."

I started to protest, but spooky as the house was, there was still an intriguing, ominous charm about it that pandered to my curiosity.

The first floor included a living and dining area plus a huge kitchen. The second floor was bedrooms, each with its own bath, and the third floor held a recreation room and three small studies. One of the watchtowers was an observatory; the other, a storage room filled with file cabinets. Ted laid his hand on the first cabinet. "We have records here going back to my grandfather. Everything having to do with the Odom family. This is Edna's bailiwick."

"She said she was your father's personal secretary. Just what all does that include?"

Holding his hands out to his side, he lifted his eyebrows. "You name it. Everything. Bookkeeping, paying bills, writing letters, researching grants. She always did a remarkable job, but now even more so since she learned to use computers."

"Oh?"

Ted's eyes laughed when he saw the puzzled frown on my face. "Hard to believe, huh? Edna was of the old school. Real leery about computers, but Dad and I finally talked her into giving them a shot. That was five or six years ago. And, like they say, the rest is history." He rapped his knuckles against the dusty cabinet. "Anytime father needed anything, he called on Edna."

I nodded, impressed.

Back downstairs on the southern corner of the mansion, he paused in front of an ornately carved door. Just inside the door, Ted stepped aside and gestured to the room. "Here it is. Just like it was when I found him." Heavy gold crosses, each about three feet long, I guessed, hung on the interior walls on either side of the door. The couch and two matching chairs were heavy and plush with richly woven fabric. Thick pillows of matching fabric trimmed with gold piping lay on the couch.

An elaborately carved desk sat before a span of windows overlooking San Madreas and San Antonio. On either side of the desk stood some sort of Oriental statues. Could have been Genghis Khan or even Tokyo Rose for all I knew.

In front of one set of bookcases sat a long table of heavy timbers, almost black from age with a lion's head standing out in relief on each panel on either end of the table. Several books were stacked on top.

The room reminded me of a gloomy old library straight from a Frankenstein movie. In fact, I might have been startled but certainly not surprised if the bookcases had opened up into a secret room.

I frowned and scanned the fairly neat room. Unlike my own apartment where papers are scattered, books lie where I tossed them and unwashed dishes fill the sinks, everything in Odom's den was stacked or filed. "I thought you searched this room for the map?"

"Oh, yes. After the police had completed their in vestigation. But I put everything back just as it was. I even looked under the carpet. Father was a stickler for neatness. Every scrap of paper, every folder had its place."

I surveyed the room.

He drew a deep breath. "I'll never forget. It was October second. I'd been out with some friends. I came in and headed for the kitchen for a nightcap." He hesitated, blinking back the tears suddenly filling his watery blue eyes. "It was almost eleven. When I passed the den,

Father's office, I saw a light under the door. I opened it to see if Father wanted to join me in a glass of wine. We often had a nighttime drink together."

I kept my mouth shut and nodded.

"He was lying right over there in front of the couch, between that end table and the coffee table. The police decided Father stumbled over the ottoman, struck his forehead against the end table, and when he bounced away, hit the back of his head on the coffee table."

I made a wry note to myself that more bouncing went on there than in a pinball machine. "And so if someone had taken the map that night, it would have had to be before eleven."

For a moment, Ted didn't reply, his attention focused on the plush red carpet between the end table and coffee table. He jerked himself back to the present. "What? Oh, yes, yes. Eleven. I stayed in the den until the police arrived thirty minutes later."

"Did the medical examiner suggest a time of death?" Ted frowned. I explained. "That might let us know just how much time the killer had to search."

"Oh." The pasty-faced man nodded. "They put his time of death around nine." He shrugged. "Something about body temperature."

That I understood. Upon death, under normal conditions, a body loses around one and a half degrees of heat per hour. If they measured body temperature at eleven-thirty or twelve, it would have lost four or five degrees.

Jotting down my notes, I asked, "Did you see anyone around that night, someone who might have wanted the map?"

"No. Edna left at seven, her normal time. I saw Father about eight when I returned his *Encyclopedia of Ancient Phoenician Maps* just before I went out for the evening, and like I said, when I came in, I stopped to see if he wanted something to drink with me. He was lying on the floor there with the encyclopedia at his side."

Studying the den, I remarked, "You searched the room thoroughly."

"After the police left. Yes."

I glanced at the pictures on the walls. "Even behind the pictures?"

He grinned. "I even took the pictures out of the frames. I'd heard about papers hidden behind paintings and that sort of thing." He chuckled and nodded to the framed crossword puzzles on the wall. "I even worked Father's crossword puzzles to see if they gave any clues."

Chuckling, I studied the various pictures. There were a couple of oils by unknown artists, several smaller frames displaying crossword puzzles, and between two floor-to-ceiling bookcases two abstract printings side-by-side, each with a single line of what appeared to be geometric symbols. I nodded to the frames. The symbols looked familiar, but I couldn't place them. "What are those?"

Print Number One

Π ⟨symbols⟩   ⟨symbols⟩   ⟨symbols⟩   ⟨symbols⟩

Print Number Two

⟨symbols⟩   ⟨symbols⟩   ⟨symbols⟩   ⟨symbols⟩

Ted frowned. "Father claimed they were ancient Egyptian puzzles from an obscure dynasty. He said no one had ever been able to translate the writing."

Egyptian puzzles? I'd never heard of that, but then all I knew about Egypt was that it was hot, and from time to time archeologists dug up mummies from the sand. I peered at the first print and grunted. "I'm not a puzzle person, but looking at these, I'd wager a guess no one will ever solve them."

He laughed. "Father was a puzzle freak."

I studied them a moment longer, unable to shake the feeling that I had seen symbols like these before, but where? One place I knew I hadn't spotted them was ancient Egypt.

In one corner of the den was a bust perched on an Ionic column. "Who's that?"

"Magellan. Father admired him for his daring explorations."

I whistled softly and looked around the den with misgiving. "Not a whole lot to work with."

He pointed to my shirt pocket where I had folded the list of names he had provided. "Any of those could have been here, and I wouldn't have known."

Or maybe you didn't want to know, I told myself, remembering the five hundred thousand dollar life insurance policy naming him beneficiary. I slipped the cards in my pocket. "That's enough for now. I'll get back with you later today. I still want to search the den myself."

Chapter Five

Edna was coming out of her office when I reached the bottom of the stairs. She smoothed the one-piece print dress she wore and then unobtrusively covered her left hand with her right. She looked up at me. "I was hoping to see you before you got away. If I can help in any way, Mr. Boudreaux, please let me know. I thought the world of Mr. Odom."

I smiled. "Thanks. I'm planning on coming back later today. I'd like to pick your brain about some of Mr. Odom's acquaintances."

She nodded primly. "Certainly. I'm here until seven."

I climbed in my pickup and turned on the air conditioning. While the cab cooled down, I studied the imposing mansion, trying to figure out just where I should start. Had the map simply been hidden well or had it been stolen?

Then I remembered the Wingate Museum of Art, the major beneficiary of Bernard Odom's will. That would be my first stop after checking in at the hotel.

Traffic in downtown San Antonio was just as congested as in Austin, the only difference being that Austin drivers gave directional signals to deliberately confuse those behind, while San Antonio drivers didn't even use them because they figured everyone was a mind reader.

A couple of blocks from the inn, my cell rang. It was Janice. Beatrice was home and resting well. "How long do you think you'll be away, Tony?"

I held my breath, wondering if she would bring up the subject of marriage again. "Hard to say, but I should be coming back regularly. It's only an hour-and-a-half drive. I'll probably be back in Saturday. I'll give you a call."

"Fine, and don't forget the next Saturday. That's the Halloween party at the Commodore Plaza."

To my relief, she punched off.

Leaving my laptop and printer in my Silverado, I checked in and went to my room. Just as I began unpacking, a knock sounded at the door. I opened it and stared into the grinning face of Jack Edney, an old pal from Austin, holding a drink in his pudgy hand.

"Hey, Tony," he gushed, waddling past me into my

room. "How's the boy? I was down on the River Walk when I spotted you drive in."

Jack and I go way back. I wasn't surprised to see him. Ever since he came into his millions, he had turned into the proverbial will-o'-the-wisp. He could turn up anywhere. In fact, he's helped me on a couple of investigations, especially the one at Bayou Teche. "What are you doing here? Where's Diane?"

Diane is my ex-wife. I ran into her in Vicksburg where she worked with the National Park Service at the battleground, and a couple of months later she was transferred to LBJ's boyhood home in Johnson City an hour or so west of Austin. I introduced her to Jack, and they'd dated some the last few months.

His pan-shaped face broke into a grin. "She's on duty, so I thought I'd take a short vacation over at the Hilton. Hard work handling those millions of dollars." His eyes glittered with laughter and a little too much booze.

I closed the door and returned to unpacking. "Poor little rich boy, huh?"

He lifted an eyebrow. "Well, like they say, it's a dirty job but somebody's got to do it." He paused and held up his glass. "Hey, how about a cool drink down at the river? I know it's cheap and vulgar, but we can sit there, drink icy drinks, and watch the women."

"Jeez, Jack. I figured all that money would change you, but you know, you're even more lecherous now than you were before."

His grin grew wider. "Yeah. Ain't that great? Now, what about that drink?"

Closing my sports bag, I shook my head. "Can't. Got a couple of stops to make. Tell you what. Is Pooky's still on the River Walk?"

"Pooky's? Yeah."

"I'll meet you there at nine. If I can make it earlier, I'll call your cell."

At four thirty, I pushed through the glass doors of the Wingate Museum of Art into a spacious lobby, on the walls of which hung numerous paintings overlooking the shiny terrazzo floor. A dozen Corinthian pedestals displaying busts of famous artists were spaced evenly about the perimeter of the lobby. Arched doorways on three walls led to various displays and exhibitions.

Unobtrusive signs on one arch pointed to the curator's office.

A young woman I guessed to be a college student looked up and smiled. "Yes, sir?"

I introduced myself. "I'm a private investigator, and I'd like to see the museum curator if he isn't busy, please."

She nodded briskly. "May I ask the purpose of your business, sir?"

Smiling amicably, I replied, "Tell him it has to do with the will of Bernard Julius Odom."

For a moment, the smile on her face froze; then quickly she rose and disappeared through the door behind her. Moments later, she opened the door and smiled. "Please. Mr. Moffit will see you now."

George Moffit reminded me of a fence post with a

hooked nose, a perfect caricature of how I always imagined Ichabod Crane in *The Legend of Sleepy Hollow*. He offered a bone-thin hand with the grip of a snail. "Mr. Boudreaux. Nice to meet you. Please, have a seat."

He sat stiffly, his eyes wary. "Now, how may I be of help?"

I'd been in the business long enough to know that individuals were always much more forthright with their answers when they knew they had a personal stake in the questioning. So, I decided to ratchet up the museum's personal stakes, so to speak. "I know the museum is included in Mr. Odom's will."

Nodding emphatically, he replied, "It was a tragedy, a terrible, terrible tragedy."

I nodded. "The reason I'm here, Mr. Moffit, is that some concerns have arisen in regard to the estate which possibly could create questions concerning the will." I held my breath, hoping I had been vague enough to raise his level of concern about the museum's place in the will.

The knit of his brows told me my little pretext had been effective.

Without giving him a chance to respond, I continued. "You've heard of the Piri Reis Map."

"Oh, yes. Bernard—I mean, Mr. Odom allowed me the honor of seeing it." He frowned, then hastily asked, "Nothing happened to the map, did it?"

I started to ignore his question but then I decided to be up front with him. Perhaps the more who knew of the missing map, the better the chance of getting a break. "Yeah. It's missing."

He gaped at me in disbelief. "Are you certain? Why, the map is invaluable."

"So I've been told. I've also been told that several individuals wanted to buy the map."

"Yes. Mr. Odom did mention that offers had been made." He shook his head. "But, he would never have parted with the map."

I pulled out the list of names Ted had provided. "For Mr. Odom to have thought so much of the museum speaks well for you as curator, Mr. Moffit." The thin man beamed. I continued blowing smoke. "That's why I have come to you. I need the opinion of a man whose judgment I can trust. Hopefully, I can gather the appropriate details to answer the questions presently posed in regard to his will."

He hesitated. "I—I don't really understand. What questions?"

I gave him a knowing smile. "I'm sorry, but I'm not at liberty to say, Mr. Moffit. I just need your help."

He nodded emphatically. "Whatever I can do, Mr. Boudreaux. Whatever I can do."

"Fine." I glanced at the list. "Do you know a man by the name of Ervin Maddox?"

His face lit. "Mr. Maddox? Certainly. He is a museum benefactor and collector of various artworks. He owns an antique shop on the River Walk. Cassandra's Baubles. He is very dedicated to his collections and an avid supporter of the museum."

"Did he know of the map?"

"Certainly." His brow knit. "Surely you don't think Mr. Maddox had anything to do with the missing map?"

"Look, Mr. Moffit. We don't know if the map was stolen or not. All we know is that it's missing. I'm visiting with everyone interested in the map, hoping one of them might shed some light on the possible location. Now, what else can you tell me about Ervin Maddox?"

He shrugged. "Not a great deal more. He's very private. Has never married from what I hear. I always had the feeling he was competing with Mr. Odom."

"Competing?"

"Yes. Attempting to build a more valuable collection, be it artwork or first editions or ancient maps." He drew a deep breath. "Mr. Odom's family has been here for generations. Mr. Maddox moved here around twenty years ago." He frowned wryly. "Sort of like the nouveau riche trying to be accepted by old money, if you know what I mean."

I knew what he meant. Ostentatious, but with a decided lack of culture. I jotted a few notes. "What about Leo Cobb? I think he and Odom worked together at times."

A faint sneer curled Moffit's lips. "Oh, yes, Mr. Cobb. Unfortunately, we need his sort. They are the ones who often come up with remarkable discoveries of art, although sometimes they take—let's see, how can I put it?—they take some license with the manner in which they acquire the piece of work. He is the one through whom Bernard purchased the Piri Reis Map."

"Any idea where he found it?"

"No." Moffit shook his head. He hesitated, staring at me as if he wanted to say more.

"And?" I prompted.

"Well, from time to time Cobb has offered the museum various artifacts, but with occasional items he could never provide a link of ownership with which I felt comfortable; consequently I purchased only a few of his goods. Five years ago, he came to me with the news of the map. I wanted it. I desperately wanted it, but I turned him down for that reason. And then I sent him to Bernard. That way, at least I would know the location of the map." He studied me for several moments. "Understand, Mr. Boudreaux. The museum and its treasures are my life. I would do all possible to protect them or any valuable artifact, such as the map, that came to my attention."

"What about Father Bertoldo Poggioreale?"

"The priest at L'Università di Grazia e la Fratellanza? I know of him. He is an expert on ancient maps, but I've never had the privilege to meet him."

The phone on his desk rang. "Excuse me." He picked up the receiver and barked into it. "I told you I was not to be disturbed, Linda. I'm quite busy on important matters for the museum." He listened another moment. "I will call him back."

He replaced the receiver and grinned sheepishly. "Forgive me. My secretary's a wonderful young student at the university. Some of our callers can intimidate her, but she'll learn."

"I understand." I glanced at the list. "Just a couple more. Joe Hogg and Lamia Odom."

"Lamia? Bernard's niece?"

I nodded.

He lifted his eyebrows. "I've met her a few times outside the museum. To my knowledge, she's never had any interest in the arts. As for Hogg, he's a wealthy man who believes buying art treasures will aid him and that wife of his to climb the rungs, so to speak, of local society. I've never been to his home, but from what I hear, he has many valuable treasures on display."

I arched an eyebrow at his expression, *that wife.* "I take it you don't approve of his wife."

A sly grin curled his lips. "You haven't met them yet, have you?"

"No."

He chuckled. "You'll know what I mean when you do."

I laughed with him. "One last question. Is there anyone else who might be able to provide me more information about these individuals?"

He pondered the question a moment, then nodded. "Rebecca Wentworth. She knows every collector, every single individual interested in the arts in San Antonio. Here, I'll give you her number."

Chapter Six

I pulled into the small parking lot at the side of the Odom mansion and walked around to the front. Moffit had given me some information to chew on. Perhaps Ted and Edna could add to it.

Ted was out but Edna showed me to the den, making small talk on the way. "This is a magnificent house," I remarked as our heels clicked on the polished heart pine floor.

"Yes. Mr. Odom's father built it. He was quite wealthy."

"Ted said Mr. Odom designed puzzles."

Keeping her left hand at her side, she opened the door. "Yes, for forty-five years." She stepped into the den and indicated four framed crossword puzzles on the wall. One was crooked. "Those are some of his."

I whistled softly. "Puzzle writing must pay good. It

probably takes a bundle to maintain such an elaborate house."

"Not all that well." She laughed and reached up to straighten the frame on the wall. I couldn't help noticing a patchy brown spot the size of a silver dollar on the back of her left hand, and I understood then why she preferred to keep it at her side. "However, he was paid more than most puzzle writers. He was quite accomplished in the art. Fortunately, his father left him well provided for."

"I see. And you've been with him . . ."

"Thirty-four years. I was going to retire in another two years and move to Lake Tahoe and all the excitement. I've always wanted to live there with the snow. Make new friends." She paused. Sadness clouded her eyes. "Looks like I won't have to wait now."

I surveyed the den. She dabbed a handkerchief at the tears filling her eyes. "He was a good man."

"That's what I've been told." It was a white lie. "Did you see him that night?"

She drew a deep breath. "Only when I was leaving. I always let him know before I left."

"At seven."

"Yes. I came up here that night, and he was sitting at his desk reading one of his favorite books, the *Dictionary of Ancient Phoenician Maps*." She paused and bit her lips. "I don't suppose I should say reading as much as studying the book. I—I—never saw him again. Alive that is."

"Do you think the map was stolen?"

She shook her head. "No. I believe he hid the map, but Teddy and I searched the den without success."

"But didn't he tell Ted that the map was in the den?"

Her slight shoulders sagged. "That's what I don't understand. He always gave the den as the location of the map." She hesitated. "Unless . . ."

"Unless what?"

Chewing on a thin lip, she thought a moment. "Mr. Odom always played with words. He loved puns. He'd laugh like a child when he ran across a particularly outrageous one."

I frowned. "I don't follow you."

Slowly, she shook her head. Not a hair in her tightly coiffed bun moved. "I'm sorry, Mr. Boudreaux. What I meant to say was—"

"Call me Tony."

"All right, Tony. I've been thinking about the map, and I can't help wondering if he really meant the map was in the den." She paused and grinned self-consciously. "Sounds foolish I guess, but he was like that. I wouldn't be surprised if he said that just to mislead Teddy. Or anyone else looking for the map."

I grimaced. "You mean, when he said it was hidden in the den, he didn't really mean it was hidden in the den?"

She lifted a tentative eyebrow. "Yes." Hesitating another moment, she shrugged. "I guess that sounds farfetched."

I studied her a moment. "Far-fetched or not, it's an interesting idea. Any thoughts on what he might have meant?"

She grimaced. "That's the problem. No idea at all."

"Did you see anyone around that night?"

Biting at her thin bottom lip, she shook her head slowly. "Not that I remember. Wait, a white car, a big one, was pulling away from the curb when I left the house."

"What kind, do you know?"

She frowned sheepishly. "I'm sorry. I don't know much about them."

"But you say that was about seven."

"A few minutes after."

"And then you went home?"

She hesitated, studying me. A faint smile played over her lips. "No. That was a special night." She grimaced. "Or, it was going to be. Don Quick. He sings the golden oldie-type songs. He had a one-night-only concert at The Clock down on the River Walk." She paused, smiling sheepishly. "I'm a big fan of his. I tried to get a picture with him, but the best I could do was one by his poster in front of the clock. I have it on my wall if you want to see it."

"Sure. When I come down. It's almost six. If you don't mind, I want to prowl around some. See what I can find. Lock the front door when you leave. I'll make sure it's locked behind me."

She glanced at the simple watch on her wrist. "That won't be necessary. Teddy will be in any time now."

I studied her another moment. "You always call him Teddy. You're not family."

She smiled shyly. "Oh no, but I almost raised Teddy

myself. His mother died in childbirth. Mr. Odom hired a nanny, but by the time she moved on a few years later Teddy and I were as close as brother and sister, although I was many years his senior."

I filed that little piece of information away in the back of my mind.

In the den, I thumbed through every book, peered at every page in every folder in the file cabinet, searched beneath every stick of furniture, unzipped every cushion and felt inside; opened up all four clocks on the walls; removed and took apart every single one of the eclectic paintings and puzzles on the wall; rapped my knuckles on Magellan's bust in case it was hollow; and checked every single pine board in the floor for any loose ones. I tore the den apart.

When I finished, I stepped back and shook my head. That map was not in the den. At that moment, Ted entered. "Any luck?"

Remembering Edna's suggestion, I replied, "No. Now tell me. Exactly what did your father say about the location of the map?"

Ted pursed his lips. "He said the location of the map was in the den."

I slipped in at Odom's desk and wrote out Ted's reply. I showed it to him. "Are you sure this is what he said. 'The location of the map was in the den.' Could he have phrased it any differently?"

He looked at me, puzzled. "That's exactly how I remember it."

"Edna came up with the idea that perhaps the map was hidden elsewhere, that the directions your father left were more of a puzzle. What do you think?"

Ted stroked his fleshy jaw, which was beginning to develop jowls. "I wouldn't put it past him, but I always assumed it was in the den. Besides, what else could 'the location of the map was in the den' mean? That's why I really believe someone stole it."

"The same one you think murdered your father?"

He looked at me forlornly. Slowly, he shook his head. "I don't know. Honestly I don't know, but that's the only thing that makes sense to me."

I indicated the four crossword puzzles on the wall. "What about those?"

"I thought of that. I worked them. They're no help."

My stomach growled. I looked at one of the clocks. Almost eight. "Well, I'm going back to the hotel. Work on some notes, and hit the ground running in the morning. I'll probably drop by around ten or so if you'll be here. I might have some more questions."

He winked. "I'll be here."

"By the way, you wouldn't happen to have Ervin Maddox's telephone number handy?"

"No, but Edna does. Let's take a look."

While Ted looked up Maddox's number and address from the telephone file on Edna's desk, I studied the wall of snapshots. There was one of Ted and an older man, whom I could tell was his father, on the porch of the mansion. Many of the pictures were candid, shots of Odom and various celebrities over the last thirty or forty years.

I found a shot of Edna riding on one of the riverboats, and another had her sitting on a bench in front of a huge, translucent clock with contrasting black stripes marking the hours. Next to her was a cardboard cutout of Don Quick. This must have been the snapshot of which she had spoken. Behind her, the clock registered the time as 8:50, ten minutes before Odom's death.

As usual, she was dressed nicely, and as usual, she had taken care to make sure that one hand covered the unsightly patch on her other.

"Here you are." I looked up as Ted handed me Maddox's address and phone number.

During the couple of hours I'd been in the Odom mansion, a front had pushed through, drying the air and dropping the temperature several degrees. I drew a deep breath of crisp air into my lungs. It would be a brisk night down on the River Walk.

I went straight from the parking lot at the Grand Isle to Pooky's, brushing past hotel signs proclaiming the upcoming Tenth Annual Bracero Festival the coming Saturday. Pooky's, a laid-back restaurant, or at least as laid-back as any other venue along the walk, was jammed between Green Chiles and Doña Margarita's. Jack was waiting at a table on the balcony overlooking the winding river, down which small pontoon boats hauled laughing tourists. He waved when he spotted me.

From the glitter filling his eyes and the jokes spilling off his lips, I figured he had spent an enjoyable afternoon drinking and watching women.

While I was never a role model for AA, the organization did help me break the habit. As much as I hate to admit it, I did indulge from time to time on special occasions. That little caveat holds true only if you considered a confrontation with my boss or the time I witnessed a beautiful woman walk into a whirling propeller as a special occasion.

When I slipped in at the table across from Jack, I noticed several different glasses on the table, all empty. When I commented on them, he announced that he was trying every drink on the menu that night. I rolled my eyes and ordered a draft beer and a side dish of pork tapas.

A couple of years back, because of a broken arm, Jack talked me into driving him to Vicksburg, Mississippi to his father's funeral. Turned out, his father had been murdered, and I helped Jack find the person responsible.

Unfortunately, the perp turned out to be Jack's sister, who managed to escape the proverbial long arm of the law; but Joe Basco, New Orleans mob boss, had a longer arm that found her on a deserted road in the middle of the swamp twenty miles south of Vicksburg.

When all of the loose ends were finally tied up, Jack Edney, ex-schoolteacher and stand-up comic on Austin's Sixth Street, was several million dollars richer.

He invested about half, dated my ex-wife, and in

general lived life however the urge struck. On two or three occasions, he even helped on some of my cases, so we had plenty to chit-chat about.

I pushed the platter of tapas across the table to him. "Have one."

He shrugged and poked one down.

I was still nursing my draft beer while Jack downed a banana daiquiri, gobbled another tapa, took on a vodka stinger, swallowed another tapa, and gulped a bourbon old-fashioned. He finished the evening with a tapa washed down with a rum sombrero cooler.

"Come on, Jack, you've had enough. I've got to do a little work tonight."

He grinned sappily and hefted his bowling ball-shaped body to his feet. He wobbled unsteadily. I took his arm. "You okay? Can you make it?"

Pulling his belly into his chest, he huffed, "Certainly. I can landle my hiquor—I mean, handle my liquor, unlike some I could men—mench—name."

I laughed. "Sure you can, Jack. Come on. I'll give you a hand. Where are you staying?"

He paused, a puzzled expression on his face. He looked up at me and blinked a couple of times in an effort to focus his eyes, but they just gazed through me. "I forget."

"What about a key?"

He looked at me blankly. "Key?"

"Yeah." I nodded impatiently. "A room key."

"Oh. Okay. Let me see." He emptied all of his pockets. No key.

For a moment, I considered tossing him in the river, but then I'd have to haul him out, and without being soaking wet, he was close to three hundred pounds.

I rolled my eyes. "Come on. Stay at my place."

Ten minutes later, I unlocked my door, flipped on the light, and froze. Someone had torn the room apart.

"What's wrong, Tony? This the right room?"

"Yeah," I muttered, staring at the tossed bed, the mattress on the floor by the patio doors, the clothes yanked from the closet, and the gear dumped from my sports bag. "Yeah, it's the right room." At least I'd taken the precaution of leaving my laptop and portable printer in my pickup.

Jack laughed drunkenly. "You sure ain't very neat." He then promptly passed out on the mattress.

Chapter Seven

After straightening the room, I left Jack snoring on the mattress on the floor, and, figuring this was one of those special occasions, went back to the River Walk for a straight bourbon.

Leaning against a balcony railing in front of Pooky's, I stared unseeing down at the thinning crowds on the flagstone sidewalks below, pondering a connection between the eighteen-wheeler earlier that morning and my tossed room.

I had worked the underbelly of society long enough to figure there was a connection even though I couldn't see it.

Ted Odom was the only one who knew I was coming down from Austin. And then he, Edna, and George Moffit were the only ones who knew I was in town. I paused, then added the police chief, Louis Ibbara, to the short list.

Ted hired me, so why would he have someone run me off the road? Besides, all three—Ted, Edna, and Moffit—knew I had learned nothing of the location of the map.

I wanted to believe that whoever broke into my room was probably some lowlife creep who made a practice of rifling tourists' rooms for whatever he could pawn, but the skeptic in me refused. I turned up the glass and drained the last of the bourbon.

That night, as I lay on a cheesecloth-covered sheet of four-by-eight plywood the hotel laughingly called box springs, I toyed with Edna's idea that the map was still in the house despite Ted's belief it had been stolen. Having thoroughly searched the den myself, my inclination was the same as Ted's. The eighteen-by-twenty-four-inch parchment was not in the den.

Staring into the darkness above my head, I blew softly through my lips. If I was going to question every individual on the list I needed background—background that might take weeks to dig out of reluctant suspects. To speed up the process, there was only one person to whom I could turn—Eddie Dyson.

Once known as Austin's resident stool pigeon, Eddie discovered his mission in life when he stumbled into the computer revolution. He discovered he possessed an uncanny knack for computers, and developed unique skills that led him to become a wildly successful entrepreneur in a seamy business.

Instead of sleazy bars and greasy money, he found his snitching niche in the bright glow of computers and credit cards. Any information I couldn't find, he could. There were only two catches if you dealt with Eddie. First, you never asked him how he did it, and second, he accepted only VISA credit cards for payment.

I never asked Eddie why he accepted only VISA. Seems like any credit card would be sufficient, but considering the value and the expediency of his service, I never posed the question. As far as I was concerned, if he wanted to be paid in kopecks, shekels or rubles, I'd pack up a couple of barrelfuls and FedEx them to him.

Failure was not a word in his vocabulary. His services did not come cheap, but he produced. With Eddie, the end was always worth the means.

Eddie was expensive, fast, and reliable.

Quickly rising and dressing, I retrieved my laptop from the pickup and using the inn's wireless, went online. In my e-mail, I asked for credit reports as well as civil and criminal background checks on Ted Odom, Edna Hudson, Lamia Sue Odom, George Moffit, and the names on the list Ted provided. And I asked for what bank accounts he could hack into.

I'm often amused when I overhear individuals discussing means to protect their own privacy. Whether we like it or not, Big Brother is alive and well. The truth is, if any Joe Sixpack wanted to part with enough palm oil, he could find out anything about anyone.

While waiting for his response, I had no choice but to plod along in my own inimitable blunder-ahead methods that had taken me years to perfect.

And I would begin with Ervin Maddox early next morning.

Jack was still snoring when I rose at five thirty. On the restaurant balcony overlooking an almost deserted River Walk, I jotted down a few questions for Maddox while I helped myself to the inn's continental breakfast of cheese bagels, chocolate doughnuts, and hot coffee, a perfect way to start off the day by clogging my arteries and loading up on the carbs.

At seven thirty, I called Maddox, simply telling him it was imperative I speak with him about the Piri Reis Map. I informed him that the map was missing, and that he and several others were known to have a more-than-casual interest in it.

I added, "I spoke with Chief Ibbara of the San Madreas police force and received his full approval to work on this case. I'm free this morning. I can be at your shop on the River Walk by eight thirty. That'll give us time before you open at nine."

Maddox hesitated. In a soft, cultured voice, he replied, "The Piri Reis Map, you say?"

"Yes."

He hesitated, then, his tone suddenly wary, asked,

"Why me? I don't know how I could be of any assistance."

"I'm talking to anyone who expressed interest in the map. Ibbara agrees that one of you might be responsible for the missing map." A little lie, which I followed with a not-too-veiled threat. "If you don't meet with me, the police might wonder why you refused."

"I beg your pardon. I didn't know anything about the map being stolen."

"I didn't say anything about it being stolen. I just said it was missing."

A sense of urgency filled his voice. "No! No! I didn't mean that. I meant, I don't know anything about the map. I wanted it, but Bernard refused to sell it to me."

"So, you wouldn't mind if I come over for a short visit and clear all of this up?"

He sighed deeply. With resignation, he asked, "Do I have a choice?"

I chuckled. "Sure you do, Mr. Maddox. Me or the San Madreas police."

After several moments, he replied, "I'm not in the shop today. You know where I live?"

"Yeah. 8135 San Jacinto Drive. I drove by last night just to be sure I could find it." The last was a lie, but I found over the years that sometimes a little white lie provides me a psychological edge if a suspect believes I've already checked him out.

I left a few minutes later so I would have plenty of time to find Maddox's place. Jack was still sleeping.

Hoping he would take the hint, I left him a note. *See you in Austin.* Jack was a good friend but he was on a drinking vacation; I was working; I didn't want him tagging after me.

Chapter Eight

As usual traffic was heavy, so I found a lane and stayed in it. Whether it was by a stroke of luck, divine intervention, or a twist of fate, a green sports car shot through a red light. I slammed on my brakes and screeched to a halt, barely missing the idiot who never slowed or looked back.

When I hit the brakes, I felt something strike the back of my loafer. I pulled across the intersection to the curb before glancing at the floorboard.

Behind my heel was a plastic bag containing white powder. "What the—" I picked up the bag. Suddenly, I clutched it in my fist and looked around hurriedly to see if anyone were watching.

I breathed a sigh of relief when I saw no one was paying me any attention. Holding the bindle in my lap,

I opened it and picked up some powder on the tip of my finger. I tasted it.

Wow! Pure coke.

For a moment, I tried to figure out what the dickens was going on. Obviously, someone had jimmied the lock during the night, planted the bindle, and locked the door. I had no idea who, although I was beginning to catch a glimmer of why. Someone wanted me out of the way and a bag of coke was just as effective as a bomb. Crushing the bag in my fist, I looked around for some way to get rid of it.

I pulled into a convenience store down the street, quickly searched the rest of the pickup, then after buying a cup of coffee used the restroom to dump the coke, flush the bag, and wash my hands. Only then did I continue on my way to Ervin Maddox's.

A few minutes after eight, I found his place, a neat brick home nestled back in a cul-de-sac lush with tropical shrubbery.

I was surprised when a slender, gray-haired gentleman who parted his hair in the middle opened the door. To add to my surprise, he smiled. He reminded me of a college professor. "Ah, Mr. Boudreaux."

"Mister Maddox?"

His smile grew wider, and he offered his hand. "Ervin."

"I'm Tony." I took his hand, taken aback by his amiable demeanor. From our conversation, I had expected him to be sullen and reticent, one from whom I would be forced to drag information.

His grip was firm, and he tugged me inside. "Come in, come in, please. I put on coffee and popped some cinnamon rolls in the oven."

Still puzzled, I followed him through the house.

A slight man, he was a couple of inches shorter than my five-ten. He wore a crisp light blue shirt, sharply pressed gray slacks, and shiny black loafers. I figured him at a hundred and forty pounds. His leather heels clicked on the hardwood floors.

The walls of the neat home were covered with a number of oil or watercolor canvases. Below the paintings on one wall was a set of glassed-in shelves spanning a forty-foot-long wall, displaying various artifacts that looked Mayan or Aztec.

I hesitated, staring curiously at a small statue sitting cross-legged with a paintbrush in one hand and a shell paint pot in the other.

Noticing my interest, he explained. "That is Pauahtun, the God of scribes and artists. The face is that of a howler monkey. He was an artisan in Mayan myth. Dates back to 725 AD or so."

"Quite a collection," I replied, admiring the hundreds of other artifacts.

"Thank you," he said simply, turning on his heel and leading the way onto a small patio out back surrounded by thick tropical shrubbery. He gestured to a padded wrought-iron chair and paused at a small table with a coffeepot. "How do you like your coffee? It's Colombian. I'm quite proud of it."

I sat. "Black is fine."

In the middle of the glass-topped, wrought-iron table was a platter covered with a starched linen cloth, beneath which, when he pulled it away, were four steaming cinnamon rolls, the hot icing running down the sides.

"Help yourself, please, Mr. Boudreaux. I'll pour." He tilted the coffeepot. "I must apologize for my rudeness when you called. I had just learned that an artifact on which I had bid had gone to another."

I studied him as he poured the coffee. He moved more like a woman—gracefully, delicately, purposefully. The truth is, he was very effeminate. On the other hand, I have been acquainted with more than my share of effeminate men whom I would never cross. "Apology accepted." Nodding to his house, I said, "Quite a collection you have in there. Have you been in the business long?"

Handing me a fragile china cup three-quarters filled with steaming black coffee, he nodded to the rolls. I declined. "I had a bagel at the hotel."

With a shrug, he poured his coffee. "As long as I can remember. Even in grade school, I collected what I, at the time, thought were treasures of art." He laughed and sat back on a cushioned chaise lounge. He grew serious. "Is what you say true—the Piri Reis Map was stolen?"

I studied him carefully, still suspicious of the change

in his demeanor. "I didn't say it was stolen, only that we can't find it."

He arched an eyebrow and with a skeptical twist on his lips replied, "If you can't find it, it's missing, and if it's missing, someone must have taken it. Right?"

I ignored his last question. "I heard you wanted the map."

"Certainly." He nodded emphatically. "But," he added with a rueful grin, "I couldn't afford it. Bernard could. That was my biggest drawback. I didn't have the funds like Bernard."

"But you were good friends."

A puzzled frown knit his brows. "Oh, no. I've never been in his house." He paused and grew insightful. Then, very composed, he continued. "I never cared for him, either professionally or personally. We weren't enemies or anything like that, but he permitted his wealth to hinder him." When I frowned, he continued. "While I consider my own collection superior to his, had I access to his funds, I could have built a world-renowned collection to which devotees of art from around the world would travel to view and admire. He was wealthy, but he lacked the taste for the truly superior objets d'art. He truly wasted much of his father's wealth on a second-rate collection."

His remarks surprised me. I thought Odom's collection truly amazing, but then I'm not an art critic. I understand only simple art like landscapes. Toss the pop art of Andy Warhol's *Campbell's Soup Cans* or the Combines of Robert Rauschenberg at me, and I'll strike out every time.

I remembered the day before at the museum when George Moffit suggested that Maddox's collection was inferior to Odom's. Of course, he also compared Maddox to the nouveau riche, but if anything, Maddox seemed a very cultured individual, and certainly not pretentious. I wondered if perhaps Moffit was a bit of a snob. "Did you and Odom collaborate in many ventures, Ervin?"

A flicker of anger flashed in his eyes. He shook his head. Then, perhaps a little too indignant, replied, "No. Even if Bernard had approached me, I wouldn't have."

"Oh? Why, if he had the money?"

He eyed me levelly. "I didn't want my reputation demeaned in any manner by inferior pieces of art. As I said, Tony, and I mean no disrespect for Bernard, he lacked that imperceptible awareness for a truly outstanding collectible."

"Does that mean the Piri Reis also?"

He shook his head emphatically. "Not by any means. The Piri Reis was, as far as I'm concerned, his greatest achievement. Personally, I envied his acquiring the map." He nodded to his house. "While my eclectic collection is truly superior to Bernard's, I must admit I have never managed such a triumphant feat."

I sipped my coffee. "You mind telling me where you were the night of October second?"

He lifted an eyebrow. "The night Bernard died?"

"Yes."

"Am I a suspect in the theft?"

With a crooked grin, I shrugged. "Along with half a dozen others." I leaned back and in a reassuring, good-old-boy tone, explained. "You see, Ervin, the easiest way for me to get a handle on who might have taken it is to know where everyone was. Now, the local cops can do it, but there's no sense in that. With me, there's no publicity, no gaping journalists anxious for a quick story on the six o'clock news."

He studied me a moment. Exuding supreme confidence, he replied, "That night I attended an exhibit at the museum, the Wingate Museum of Fine Art. There was an exhibit of the four navigational maps of Christopher Columbus followed by a fascinating discourse on the history of the maps. The exhibit and lecture began at seven and ended at ten."

I pursed my lips. "That was over two weeks ago. How can you be so certain?"

He smiled sadly. "Usually Bernard attends the museum's exhibits. I had noticed he was not there. The next morning, I heard the news."

"I see. You have witnesses naturally."

"Oh yes. We signed in and Rebecca Wentworth wished us a good night. You can check with her."

I sipped the coffee. "You mentioned you didn't care for him either professionally or personally."

He knit his brows and pursed his lips. "Bernard was a hard man. Treated those about him like cattle, even family and employees. I could tell you he was selfish, self-centered, and arrogant beyond belief, but you'll probably find that out for youself." He paused. "I don't like to speak ill of the dead, but Bernard Odom had no more feeling or compassion for those about him than that statue of Pauahtun in the living room."

With my note cards in hand, I sat in my pickup studying the neat house. I liked Ervin Maddox. He was different, but then we all are. And I wanted to believe him. From what I saw of him and his house, he didn't seem like the ostentatious cretin George Moffit had described.

On the other hand, I was still puzzled by the change in his manner. Was he sincere? Or was it simply for my benefit?

Quickly, I jotted down the interview on the cards, then headed for the nearest McDonald's for a cup of coffee at the drive-thru.

With my coffee, I parked in the shade of one of the tall elm trees lining the restaurant lot. I called Rebecca Wentworth who graciously agreed to see me. "But I must leave for a book signing by eleven."

Twenty minutes later, I pulled up to the curb in front of a sprawling white brick overlooking Coldwater Creek. Wentworth met me at the door, a petite woman wearing an attractive pale blue dress that left no doubt that she worked out regularly. She led me into the den.

Sliding into the chair she indicated, I jumped right into the interview. "I appreciate you working me in to your rushed schedule, so I won't waste any of your time.

I'm looking into the disappearance of the Piri Reis Map."

She grimaced. "I couldn't believe it when I heard. Bernard's death, and then the map going missing . . . Truly, truly terrible. Why, once Bernard even hinted he might give the map to the museum."

I frowned. "Really? Mr. Moffit didn't mention that."

With a warm chuckle, she replied, "Oh, Bernard didn't say anything to George about it. He just mentioned it to me in passing. That was a couple of years ago. He asked me not to say anything just in case he decided not to donate the map."

"What kind of person was Mr. Odom?"

She frowned. "Kind of person?"

"Yes. Easy to get along with? That sort of thing."

She gave a wry chuckle. "There's no way you can say Bernard was easy to get along with." She paused, then with a crooked smile, added, "But he was rich. A museum can tolerate a great deal, Mr. Boudreaux, from the rich."

"So"—I gave a matching smile—"he wasn't the kind of person you'd want to work for."

"Not me." She laughed, shaking her head.

"I see. I just talked to Ervin Maddox. He said he was at the Christopher Columbus exhibit you hosted on October second at the museum."

She nodded and a faint sneer erased her becoming smile. "He was."

"The entire time?"

A frown wrinkled her forehead. "I think so. Ervin is

sly. He's one of those little men hungry for attention. He shows up at all the exhibits. Stays the whole time. Prowls the buffet, looking for anyone to talk to." She paused. Her brows knit. "I don't dislike the man, Mr. Boudreaux. I feel sorry for him. He is so desperate to be accepted that he always goes too far. He's the kind of, well, pest you cannot keep from seeing, even if you don't want to."

"So he was there?"

"Yes."

"Did he ever leave?"

"That"—she lifted an eyebrow—"I can't say."

I considered her words. "I just spoke with Mr. Maddox. He seemed pleasant enough, not pushy."

With the tip of her tongue in her cheek, she looked at me with amusement. "As I said, he is sly. He is quite adept at covering his feelings. Once, he became outraged that Bernard Odom was keynote speaker for an exhibit I was hosting. You see, he owns Cassandra's Baubles on the River Walk. Consequently, he considers himself an expert in all fields. He felt that he would be a better speaker, and then demanded to know why he was always ignored. I told him I didn't ignore him. It was just that Mr. Odom was better qualified." She paused and rolled her eyes. "Well, sir, he exploded. He never laid a finger on me, but the violence of his temper frightened me. It still does, although in all fairness to him, I have never seen him display it again."

"So you don't know if he left the museum that night or not?"

"No. But, I know how you can find out." She rose quickly and disappeared into the next room. When she returned, she handed over a VHS tape. "I always videotape my exhibits." The smile on her face turned into one of grim resolve. "I've been in this business long enough to discover that many who attend exhibits are not above—well, I don't want to say stealing, but—"

"Purloining."

Her eyes laughed. "I prefer to say *borrowing*. You'd be amazed at what a deterrent security cameras are."

"I can imagine," I replied, taking the tape.

"The video is of the Columbus exhibit. All other wings of the museum were closed to our visitors. The room at the end of the hall is where the lecture took place."

"Thank you. One other question. Have you ever been in Mr. Odom's home?"

She nodded. "On a few occasions."

"On the wall in his den are two abstracts, a line of characters Ted says are Egyptian puzzles."

Wentworth lifted a skeptical eyebrow. "That was Bernard. He claimed it was obscure writing from an obscure dynasty." She paused. "It might be, but I'd never seen anything like it."

At that moment, her doorbell rang. She glanced at the door. "I'm sorry, but that's my ride."

"No problem. Can I get back in touch with you?" I asked as we headed for the door. "There are two or three other folks I have questions about."

"Certainly. In fact, take down my cell number. Give

me a call from your car. The drive to the library takes about fifteen or twenty minutes. I can talk on the way."

After her limo drove away, I climbed in my pickup. Before I could punch in her number, two San Antonio police cruisers pulled up, one in back and one in front of me.

Now, the bindle of coke made sense.

So I was not surprised when, moments later, they began searching my pickup.

Chapter Nine

After thoroughly searching both me and my pickup, one of the officers returned my driver's license and apologized. "Sorry to inconvenience you, Mr. Boudreaux, but we had a tip a vehicle bearing your license number was transporting illegal contraband."

I grinned at them. "No problem." I explained my job in San Antonio, and added, "This sort of thing has been going on the last couple of days." When they frowned, I continued, relating the incident with the eighteen-wheeler the previous morning and my tossed room last night. I did not mention the coke. "If you want, you can contact Chief Ibbara in San Madreas. He'll verify who I am."

After the cruisers left, I muttered a soft curse. Wentworth was at her signing, probably wondering why I hadn't called. I glanced at my watch. 12:30.

I decided to go back to the inn, grab some lunch up in my room and watch her video.

To my dismay, Jack Edney was waiting for me in the lobby. His usual ebullient self, he hefted himself from his chair, rolled across the lobby to me, and grabbed my arm. "Hey, Tony, appreciate you putting me up last night. I didn't know where I was this morning. I must have had a lot to drink last night. Last I remember was a banana daiquiri."

"You had half a dozen more after that."

He shook his head. "Well, come on. I'll buy us lunch. I'm starving."

"Can't." I held up the tape. "Got to watch this."

A leering grin curled his fat lips. "Porno, huh?"

"Not quite."

"Well, I'll watch with you."

"I thought you were hungry."

"We'll call room service. I'll pay."

Twenty minutes into the video, Jack grunted, pushed to his feet, and, grabbing his hamburger and beer, announced he was going down to the River Walk. "You can stay up here and watch that boring stuff if you want."

I chuckled. "See you later."

Rebecca Wentworth had nailed one thing about Ervin Maddox: he never strayed too far from the buffet, although he indulged himself in very little of its fare. I don't think a single guest going through the line escaped him.

Jack was right. The video would win no Oscar as a thriller, but about forty-five minutes or so after Jack left, Maddox, wearing a tweed jacket with leather elbows, disappeared through an arch leading to the restrooms. As minutes passed, and he didn't return, I began to wonder.

An hour later, he emerged from the arch. An hour in the bathroom? Not likely. Maddox had lied. Why?

A thought hit me. I dialed George Moffit at the museum. "One fast question," I said. "Does the arch leading to the restrooms by the Columbus exhibit lead anywhere else in the museum?"

"Why yes," he replied, clearly puzzled. "The hallway leads to the front lobby."

I thanked him and hung up, wondering just where Maddox had spent that hour. Still, there might be a logical explanation for his absence.

I dialed Maddox's home number. When he answered, I asked, "Did you, by any chance, leave anytime during the exhibit at the museum on the second?"

He hesitated. "No. I parked my car in the museum garage. I even have receipts with time in and time out if you wish to see them."

His last remark took me by surprise. "Receipts. Do you make it a practice to keep parking lot receipts?"

In a surprised voice, he said, "Why yes, doesn't everyone? Business deductions."

After hanging up, I studied the video on the TV. What if he had left by another means?

Quickly I began dialing local taxi services.

By the time the three-hour video ended, I had discovered that a cab company had picked up a fare in front of the museum at eight thirty and dropped it off at 2112 Fairchild, and another company had picked up a fare at that same address but had no record of where the fare was taken, or when he'd been dropped off.

I hesitated. 2112 Fairchild. Odom's place! My pulse picked up. I was on to something. "Isn't that unusual?" I asked the dispatcher in regard to the destination of the second fare.

"Yeah, but not with this joker. Casey would forget his head if it wasn't tied on. But he's dependable for the most part. Ain't much of that around no more."

"How can I get in touch with this Casey?"

"Can't. He's on a fishing trip. He'll be back Saturday. He's scheduled to work Sunday."

"Good. Can I leave my name and number?"

After hanging up, I leaned back and stared at the wall, wondering if that fare could have been Maddox.

I rewound the tape to the point Maddox came back into the picture. I replayed it noting the time on my watch. An hour later, the exhibit closed down. An hour. If the museum closed the exhibit at ten then Maddox didn't return until nine o'clock.

"That would work," I muttered, jotting the new information on my note cards. "Fifteen minutes there, fifteen minutes inside, and fifteen minutes back to the museum."

Before I confronted him, I would show the cab drivers a picture of Maddox and see if they could identify him.

I paused, shaking my head as a cynical thought crept into my head. Perhaps that's why he pulled such a switch in behavior. He didn't want me snooping into his business.

A sudden yawn overtook me. I hadn't slept much the night before. Jack's snoring didn't help; nor did the clamor from the River Walk; nor did the fact I lay awake pondering the missing map.

Yawning again, I stretched my arms over my head and lay back on the bed. Moments later, I was asleep. I awakened around eight that evening, showered, slipped into fresh clothes and started for the door. As an afterthought, I booted up the laptop and went online.

A big grin spread over my face when I spotted mail from Eddie Dyson.

I printed up his information and cringed when I saw his charges. Seven hundred dollars. I thumbed through the sheath of papers. While he had been unable to provide all of the information, that which he did was detailed. I printed it.

"It's worth it," I muttered, shutting down the computer and heading for the door. I was looking forward to a leisurely Mexican dinner washed down with an icy margarita while I perused the information from Eddie.

Hoping to avoid Jack so I could get some work done, I turned the other way on the River Walk and found a balcony table at Pepe's, known for his sumptuous dinners of shredded beef chimichangas and his high-powered margaritas.

I sat back and drew a deep breath, enjoying the tropical ambiance of gay voices, laughing faces, and the occasional come-hither look flashed by dark, daring eyes.

After the young waitress took my order, I opened the manila folder in which I had placed Eddie's report and began reading. To my disappointment, he had not been able to procure all of the bank accounts.

A few minutes later, the waitress slid an icy margarita in front of me followed by a platter of steaming chimichangas, but I was too absorbed in Eddie's report.

My eyes grew wide. I whistled softly. By the time I finished the report, my dinner was cold, my drink warm. Not a good combination.

Ordering another margarita, I apologized to the waitress and asked her to warm my dinner. I grinned sheepishly and tapped a finger on the manila folder. "I just got involved in work. Sorry."

I had hoped Eddie would provide me something to chew on. He did but it was a piece of leather. Of the eight names I sent Eddie, five had no obvious motive.

Ted Odom had no reason to steal the Piri Reis. The map belonged to him. And nothing in Edna Hudson's nor Father Poggioreale's report suggested motive, although I was curious as to why, according to Ted and Edna, the good Father tried to buy it three times.

The fourth one, Joe F. Hogg, appeared to be nothing more than a newly rich man struggling for the celebrity his wealth might bring. Other than his having married a Las Vegas showgirl two years earlier, there was nothing unusual about him. Many individuals, after gaining wealth, turned to the arts, hoping some of the sophisticated culture would somehow soften the crassness of money.

And the last was George Moffit, curator of the museum for forty years, well respected, happily married to the same woman for thirty-eight years, and earning a respectable income from the museum. He wanted the map for his second wife, the museum, but even if he had stolen the Piri Reis, where would he display the map? An understandable quirk among museum curators is that they want to display their artifacts for the world to see and admire.

Opening the folder, I started rereading files on the other three, this time circling important facts with a ballpoint.

Most of the details Eddie provided for Ervin Maddox, owner of Cassandra's Baubles on the River Walk, I had uncovered except for the fact his bank account was running low. From Maddox's own admission, he wanted the map, but its value was beyond his grasp.

Art broker Leo Cobb had been booked twenty-two years earlier for the theft of a Seventeenth Dynasty alabaster unguent vase, but the case was dropped upon the return of the vase, for the museum in Seattle did not want the publicity. Cobb, Bernard Odom's one-time liaison with hopeful sellers of various artifacts, had sued Odom three times, twice for breach of contract and once for slander. He'd won one and lost two, the latter a slander case four years earlier.

According to Eddie's report, Cobb had filed for bankruptcy only a year earlier. I frowned, noting that while his income dropped after the last suit against Odom, it didn't appear enough to have precipitated bankruptcy. But even now, his mortgage company was threatening to foreclose on his home.

I whistled softly. That was motive in spades, plus, as an art broker, he had connections with buyers all over the world.

The young waitress interrupted me with my margarita. I sipped it quickly, not waiting for it to water down into the bland taste of the first.

After she left, I pulled out Eddie's report on Lamia Sue Odom. I shook my head as I scanned the report. She was well traveled, having visited over thirty countries and spending three-quarters of her life since her fifteenth birthday in Europe.

True, she was beneficiary to a half-million-dollar policy on Bernard Odom, but at a glance at her bank account, I could tell five hundred thousand wouldn't last her more than a couple of years. Five million, ten million for the Piri Reis would provide her another twelve, fifteen years on the jet-set circuit.

A young man appeared at my side with a steaming platter of freshly prepared chimichangas packed with shredded pork and the oven-baked flour tortilla basted with pineapple. I put the folder aside, determined to push the map from my mind and enjoy my meal.

I took a bite of the piping hot chimichanga. I looked up at the sound of laughter. Beyond the laughing foursome at the next table, I spotted Ted Odom speaking with two hard-looking zombies on the River Walk, his face showing a sense of urgency.

Easing my head to one side, I peered around the back of an animated young woman whose bouncy energy kept blocking my view, but even a fleeting glance at the two goombahs confronting Ted told me they were not deacons of the local church. At that moment, I would have given hundred-to-one odds they were soldiers belonging to Patsy Fusco, San Antonio's resident mob boss.

The young woman leaned back. I stared at her unseeing, wondering. Ted and those two were like oil and water. They didn't go together, so what was the conversation all about? Why did he look so worried?

A sharp jab on my shoulder jerked me back to the present. I shook my head and looked up into the glowering face of an angry giant. "Huh? Oh, yeah. What's up?"

He hooked a thumb at the table next to us. "I don't like nobody staring at my wife like you was."

The three at the table next to me were glaring daggers. I blinked my eyes once or twice, then forced a weak grin. "Sorry, pal. I wasn't staring at your wife. I just got to thinking about my job, and was staring into space."

He glared at me, confused by my apology. He glanced at his wife.

I turned to the young woman. "I apologize if I offended you, ma'am."

She nodded, and he grunted. "Well, okay."

By then, Ted had disappeared.

I leaned back and stared at the folder on my table, my curiosity piqued.

Back at the Grand Isle Inn, I paused before pushing my door open, half expecting the room to be tossed again. It was as I had left it. Not even Jack Edney was around to greet me.

I stepped onto the balcony and called Danny O'Banion, Austin's local mob boss. Danny and I have a history, all the way back to high school.

Very few people can place a call and get through to Danny. I'm one of the few. I don't know if that says much for my character or not, but it does provide me a means of information that I might not be able to find elsewhere.

Danny finally came on. After a couple of minutes of idle chit-chat, I asked if he could contact Patsy Fusco and see what he knew about a guy named Ted Odom.

"Trouble, Tony?" The tenor of his question told me he would send help if I needed it.

I grinned. "No. Just a case. No trouble. I got a feeling Odom might be involved with Fusco, that's all. Nothing to do with Fusco."

"No problem. Same cell number?"

"Same one."

After hanging up, I called Leo Cobb. I was anxious to

see why he had filed suit against Odom three times. A woman who identified herself as Mrs. Cobb answered. Her husband was not in.

I thanked her and hung up, but something about her strained voice made me wonder.

Chapter Ten

As cynical as it sounds, people tell lies. Some white, some not so white. Al Grogan works on the assumption that every individual he interviews is lying. Working on that basis, you quickly learn to verify information at least once, and twice if possible.

So that was my mindset when I called Leo Cobb just after eight the next morning. The same woman informed me that he was on a business trip to Panama City, Florida for the next week.

I feigned disappointment. "Looks like I goofed. I should have called him when I got in town day before yesterday." I waited for her response.

"Oh," she replied brightly. "That wouldn't have done you any good. He's been gone a week already."

After hanging up, I called Joe Hogg.

Hogg lived in Ridglea Hills, a gated community north of San Antonio filled with two-million-dollar mansions on two-acre grounds, each with a tennis court and swimming pool.

Pulling into the parking area at the side of the house just after nine, I quickly skimmed back through Eddie's report on Hogg. The guy was worth millions, had a maid, a chauffer, and a trophy wife. In his garage sat a white Cadillac, a gray Rolls Royce, and a bright red Ferrari. "Not too shabby," I muttered under my breath.

A neatly attired Hispanic maid showed me to the sunroom overlooking the pool. Hogg, wearing plaid slacks and a white Polo shirt stretched tight over a protruding belly that would never fit behind the wheel of that red Ferrari, rose and with an ebullient grin removed a black cigar from his lips and offered his hand. "Mr. Boudreaux," he said, looking up at me. "We've been expecting you." Using the cigar as a pointer, he indicated the sultry blond standing at his side, a head taller than the short man. "This is my wife, Nadine."

Nadine Hogg was a striking blond wrapped in a filmy house robe. Voluptuous would not do her justice. She smiled halfheartedly, and just as halfheartedly offered me her hand. "Mr. Boudreaux."

I didn't know if she wanted me to kiss it or shake it, so I simply shook it. "Mrs. Hogg." I suppressed a grin when I wondered just how the beautiful woman in front of me managed to tolerate the surname.

Had I been stuck with that surname I would have changed it as fast as I could, and even if I didn't, I certainly would never have named my daughter Ima as did Texas Governor George Hogg.

With a nod, she lowered herself into a chair.

The sunlight reflecting off his balding head, Hogg gestured to a wrought-iron chair across the table from Nadine. He nodded to the silver platter in the middle of the table. "What'll you have—coffee, juice, tea?" He laughed. "Sorry, no booze. Too early."

His wife rolled her eyes.

He was loud and boisterous in an amiable sort of way, and I could see why he had managed to build such a chain of car lots. "Coffee's fine."

The maid, her dark face impassive, appeared out of nowhere and poured me a cup of coffee. As she turned to leave, Nadine stopped her. "You can take my cup, Carmen. I'm finished."

Carmen nodded perfunctorily. "Yes, ma' am."

Jack nodded to her retreating back. "She's good help, Boudreaux. That's hard to find today, you know?"

I didn't but I nodded anyway. "That's what I hear."

He paused, then grew serious. The cigar bobbing between his lips, he said, "When you called earlier, you said the Piri Reis Map was missing. Stolen?"

Before I could reply, Nadine rose.

Hogg snapped. "Where do you think you're going?"

She looked around at him with a hint of disdain. "If you remember, you insisted I help the Ladies' Club plan for the Fall Fashion Show. I have to dress. We need to go over our final plans and make sure we have help with serving at the show next Monday."

He grunted. "Serving? Take Carmen."

She looked at him in frustration. "Monday is Carmen's day off, remember?"

"So? Pay her double."

"I've already asked. Remember? I told you yesterday." She shook her head. "You never hear a word I say."

"Oh. Yeah. I remember. Well, go on." He nodded at me. "Say good-bye to Mr. Boudreaux."

Nadine glared at him, lifted her shoulders, and in a honeyed voice said, "Very pleased to have met you, Mr. Boudreaux."

She strode majestically from the sunroom. Hogg shrugged and grinned sheepishly. "You got to excuse her. She came out of Las Vegas where she was a showgirl. She's still got some manners to learn." He flicked his cigar ashes on the terrazzo floor.

I grinned reassuringly. "You're teaching her well."

He beamed at my compliment. "Well, I try to teach her right. I ain't no—what is it?—role model, but I know good manners when I see them."

"I'm sure you do."

"So, back to the map. No idea what happened to it, huh?"

"That's why I'm here. I'm talking to everyone who expressed an interest in it." Quickly I added, "You might know something that will help."

He shrugged. "Sure. What do you need to know?"

I pulled out my note cards and pretended to read from one. "You have tried to buy the Piri Reis several times. Why?"

Removing the cigar from his lips, he knit his brows in concentration. "You much into collecting artworks, Boudreaux?"

I shook my head. "Not much."

"Well, I am. I'm trying to build a quality collection." With his cigar between his fingers, he made a sweeping gesture that included all of the United States and half of Europe. "A collection with enough class that art lovers and critics from around the world will want to see it."

Lifting an appreciative eyebrow, I said, "Quite a challenge."

He jabbed the cigar back in his lips. "Yeah, but I started from nothing. I worked my keister off while people laughed at me. Now I'm worth over ten million bucks. By next year, I'll double it. Not bad, huh?"

"Not bad at all, Mr. Hogg. Not bad at all. So that's why you wanted the Piri Reis?"

He frowned. "Certainly. Why else? From all I heard, it is one of the most valuable maps in the world. What joker wouldn't want it in their collection? It would be the crowning achievement for any collector."

"I'm curious, Mr. Hogg. Your collection of art, the paintings, sculptures, various artifacts from different periods of ancient history, all of those—you will enjoy them during your life. What do you do then, donate to museums and libraries?"

"Not me. Soon as I can, I'm donating my entire collection and the funds to the university that will build a museum of art and name it after me. After all, those that got it needs to think about helping educate them that don't. Right?" He stared at me, waiting for a response. He stared off into space and stretched both arms over his head. "Can't you see it? The Joe and Nadine Hogg Museum of Fine Art. Got a nice ring, huh?"

For a moment, his audacity took me aback, but I re minded myself I was talking to a used car salesman. Audacity was his forte, his way of life, and who could argue with the man? He was worth over ten million dollars.

But the title—The Joe and Nadine Hogg Museum of Fine Art—somehow did not resonate with the cultural synergy of the Metropolitan Museum of Art or the Bonaventure Museum of Fine Art. Of course, they could call it Hogg's Museum of Art or simply Hogg's Museum, although both names resounded with the same grating implication as the name, Hogg Pen.

"Good idea."

"Yep. That way, long after Nadine and me has kicked off, we'll be remembered."

I nodded again. "I have no doubt. By any chance, did you attend the exhibit on the navigational maps of Christopher Columbus at the Wingate Museum of Art on October second?"

"The night Odom croaked?"

I nodded.

"Not me." He studied me for a moment. "I don't go to that stuff. I got the money to buy it, and that's what I do and will keep on doing."

I frowned. "So, how do you determine the quality of your purchase?"

He looked at me like I was crazy and shook his head. "Why, by what my brokers tell me, naturally. How else?"

"And you trust your brokers to be honest with you?"

Hogg snorted and shook his head. "From what I pay those suckers, they'd better be," he said with a harsh laugh.

"I understand that. So, if you weren't at the exhibit, do you mind telling me where you were?"

His eyes narrowed. He studied me for several moments. "You don't figure I took the map, do you?"

I sensed a hidden challenge in his tone. "Stop and think about it, Mr. Hogg. If one of your car lots came up short on funds, and only five of your people handled the money, who would you suspect?"

He glared at me, his face growing red. "You figure I took the map?" Before giving me a chance to answer, he added, "For your information, I didn't take the map. I wanted it but I didn't take it. I don't have to steal nothing. I can buy anything I want. You hear me?"

I was ready to believe him until his green eyes darted nervously to the silver coffeepot on the table, and he dragged the tip of his tongue across his lips. He was covering something. The signs were obvious, or I was blind. "So, you won't mind telling me where you were that night."

"I was here, all night. Ask my wife."

With a wry grin, I replied, "Believe me, Mr. Hogg. district attorneys don't consider wives reliable witnesses."

"All right, then. Ask the maid, Carmen. She'll tell you I didn't leave the house."

"Sorry. I can't ask her."

His brows knit, furrowing his forehead with deep wrinkles. With a trace of belligerence, he snorted, "Why not?"

"Because she wasn't here, was she? Your wife, Mrs. Hogg, said the maid has Mondays off, and October second was a Monday."

He stared at me, speechless.

I had him off-balance, so I remarked, "I noticed you have a new Cadillac in the garage."

Slowly, he nodded, a puzzled expression on his face. "Yeah. I got it about three weeks ago. That ain't no crime, is it?"

I took a wild guess. "No, but maybe you can explain what you were doing in front of Odom's house that Monday night. You were seen pulling away from the curb."

He stared at me defiantly for several seconds, and then his gaze wavered.

In my gut, I knew he was lying. I smiled disarmingly and put on a little more pressure. "Come on, Mr.

Hogg. I know you were at the house. I've got an eye-witness who saw your Cadillac at the curb."

His eyes narrowed, and then he drew a deep breath. "All right. All right, so I was there."

Chapter Eleven

He stared at me for several seconds. I could see tiny wheels in his brain whirling frantically, the gears failing to mesh. He grimaced. "Yeah, I got there about seven forty-five or so, but I didn't go in the house. I went there to make a final offer on the map. I sat in the car a few minutes, then decided not to. I drove away."

"Drove away? Before seeing Odom?"

"Yeah. Hey, I know it sounds screwy, but that's what I did."

With a wry edge on my words, I remarked, "I suppose your chauffeur will verify that?"

"Naw. I drove myself."

"Then explain something to me, Mr. Hogg. If you wanted the map so bad, why did you go to all the trouble to drive over there, and then leave without making another offer?"

Despite the air conditioning, sweat rolled down his rotund cheeks. A look of desperation filled his eyes. "Look, I got pride. I'd made so many offers, I knew the old man wouldn't take a new one. I was frustrated, so I sat there in the car and just suddenly got fed up with the map and all its hoopla." Anger replacing the defiance in his eyes, he paused and glared at me, daring me to dispute his words. "And that's all there is to it."

"Where did you go from there?"

"Down to the Alamo Sports Bar. The Jets-Buffalo game started at eight. I'd laid some money on it. You can ask Calvin Landreth. He owns the place."

I smiled amicably. "No problem then. Tell me," I said, changing the subject, "being the connoisseur of art you are, do you know of anyone who might have wanted the Piri Reis enough to steal it?"

The anger in his eyes diminished. He pondered my question. "In case you haven't noticed, I'm not no connoisseur. And to answer your question, I don't know anybody who would steal it."

"What do you know of Ervin Maddox?"

He arched an eyebrow and grinned crookedly. "Maddox? Yeah, he owns an antique store on the River Walk. He fancies hisself an expert on artifacts. Always spouting off about them."

"You ever do business with him?"

"At times."

"What about Leo Cobb? You ever do business with him?"

Hogg grew wary. "Sometimes. Depends on the item."

"Do you think Cobb or Maddox might have taken the Piri Reis?"

He considered the question a moment. "What are they going to do with it? They can't put it on display."

"What about a private collection?"

"Sure." He snorted. "But what's the sense in having a piece of history like that that no one can see it except you?"

I lifted an eyebrow. "Just the fact you have it?"

A cynical grin played over his lips. "That ain't my style."

That, I could understand. I rose and slipped my note cards in my pocket. "That's all I needed to know, Mr. Hogg. I certainly appreciate your time."

I paused at the end of Hogg's drive before pulling into the street. A black limo with dark windows sat next to the curb a block away. I thought nothing of it until moments later when I pulled up to a signal light and the limo stopped behind me.

A goombah who could have been a body double for the Incredible Hulk in a thousand dollar Nicky Hilton suit tapped on my window.

Reluctantly, I rolled it down a couple of inches. "Yeah?"

"You Tony Boudreaux?"

I started to get cute, but I glanced at his massive fist, which, I kid you not, was the size of the head of a forty-pound catfish out of a Louisiana bayou. Not a car window existed that could survive its force. I nodded. "Yeah."

He grunted. "Patsy Fusco wants to see you. Follow us."

Through the side view mirror, I watched him lumber back to the limo. I could have sworn the ground trembled.

I waited until the limo passed and pulled in behind. Danny O'Banion had worked fast.

Patsy Fusco rose from behind his desk when I entered. A slender, neatly attired man, he looked more like an aristocratic senior model for *Gentleman's Quarterly* than a mob boss. He smiled warmly and offered his hand. "Ah, Mr. Boudreaux. Danny called me about you. Good man, that O'Banion. You two know each other long?"

I quickly outlined our history back to high school and added, "I appreciate you seeing me, Mr. Fusco."

He laughed and slapped me on the shoulder. "Patsy, Tony. All my friends call me Patsy. You're a friend of O'Banion, and he's a friend of mine, so that makes us friends, right?"

Although I had known him all of one minute, who was I to argue with his logic? "Right."

He gestured to a chair in front of his desk. "Have a seat, Tony." He glanced at one of his soldiers. "Joey, bring me a glass of tomato juice. How about you, Tony?

What'll you have? I'm not a drinking man, but we have beer and whiskey if you want it."

"No, thanks. Tomato juice is fine."

Fusco nodded, his expression showing his approval of my choice of drinks. His man disappeared. The dapper mobster leaned back and pressed his steepled fingers against his lips. "So, Danny says you got a question about some citizen named Ted Odom."

"You know him?"

Fusco shrugged. "I don't know." That was his way to suggest I tell him more, so I brought him up to date on the missing map.

"I'm in the middle of trying to figure out what happened to it. I spotted Odom talking to a couple of guys last night on the River Walk who looked like, well, to be honest, looked like soldiers. It made me wonder if there was more going on with Odom than I knew."

He cut his eyes over his steepled fingers at his man. "Send Little Augie to me."

Moments later, a well-dressed man about five-six and sporting kinky black hair entered. Without a glance in my direction, he said, "You sent for me, Patsy?"

"Yeah. Any of your boys know a bozo by the name of Odom?"

Augie shrugged. "Odom? Yeah, Boss. One plays the nags. The other is a small-time stringer."

"Which one is Ted Odom?"

Augie nodded, his kinky hair bobbing. "The nags. Five, ten Gs at a time."

"He up to date?"

"Yeah, Boss. He always pays on time."

Fusco looked at me and raised his eyebrows as if to ask "Anything else?"

I addressed the mob boss. "A long-timer?"

"Ten years at least, Boss," Augie said, still not looking in my direction.

"What about the other one?" Fusco asked.

Little Augie shrugged. "An eyeful. Charley Blue is her candy man. She ain't nothing to us, Boss. Small change."

Which meant that what little Lamia Sue Odom made selling drugs was not worth Patsy Fusco's concerning himself. I pushed to my feet. "That tells me all I need to know, Patsy. Thanks."

He nodded. "Anything for a friend. Tell Danny hello when you see him."

"You got it."

My stomach growled as I pulled back into the traffic. It was almost noon and my morning bagels and coffee were down to my toes. I stopped at one of the ubiquitous McDonald's, grabbed a burger, fries and soft drink, and pulled into the shade of the giant oaks and elms in Brackenridge Park off the old Austin Highway.

While I ate, I considered where I was. Ervin Maddox had the opportunity. His whereabouts were unaccounted for around the time of the theft. Motive? Jealously initiates many regrettable and foolish acts.

Hogg? With him it was ego, a drive, a desire to possess that which no one else could. And he was, by his own admission, in the area around seven forty-five that night.

Ted Odom, while he had opportunity, appeared to have had little motive, for he was current in his debts. So he played the horses? He would soon be coming into half a million and if we found it, the map.

And then there was the niece, Lamia Sue, who had an apartment at the Elena Towers on the River Walk. I paused and studied the name, Lamia. Unusual, but in the back of my mind it struck a chord of familiarity. And then I remembered. The ancient Greeks believed that Lamia, a snake-like creature with a human head and breasts, was a vampire who stole little children to drink their blood. I shivered. Some reference.

I had yet to speak with Cobb, who, according to his wife, was out of town. From the few opinions I'd solicited, no one held him in high regard. And according to Eddie's report, Cobb had sued Odom three times.

In our earlier conversation that morning, Cobb's wife had mentioned he had been out of town for a week. Suddenly I remembered two days earlier a remark Edna made to Ted that Cobb had called and wanted to stop by. She also stated she told Cobb the map was missing and Ted had hired a private investigator to find it.

Two curious questions popped into my mind. One, why was it none of the other suspects were out of town—only Cobb? And second, if Cobb had been in Florida for a week, how could he drop by the Odom mansion that morning?

Only one answer. Cobb was home, and his wife was lying for him. But, why was she lying? Had Cobb stolen the Piri Reis for another buyer? That was a logical guess. He brokered items of art, of historical value. I chuckled. I'd let Cobb think I'd fallen for his little pretext. But then, I had a little pretext of my own for him.

Twenty minutes later, I pulled up to the curb in an older and once-prestigious neighborhood. Cobb's house was a two-story, red brick with white mortar and gabled roof and white columns with Corinthian capitals.

A sidewalk ran the length of the neighborhood, which I guessed was developed back in the fifties and sixties. Most of the lawns were neat, edges trimmed, weeds pulled. One or two homes were up for sale.

I drove slowly to the end of the block and back, deliberately studying each house. I stopped in front of the Cobb house, climbed out of my pickup, dropped to my knees and started searching through the grassy lawn.

Chapter Twelve

Cats aren't the only creatures driven by curiosity. From time to time as I dug through the grass, I noticed neighbors staring at me. From the corner of my eye, I caught movement of a curtain in the front window of the Cobb house.

Finally, curiosity proved too much for Mrs. Cobb, and she came onto the porch. Several pounds overweight, the short woman wore black tights and a baggy white shirt that hung to mid-thigh. Her brown hair was cut short. "You. In my yard. What are you doing?"

Feigning distress, I looked up. "Ma'am?"

"I said what are you doing in my yard?"

Climbing to my feet, I brushed off my knees and approached her. "I'm sorry. I should have asked first, but, well, last night my fiancé and I had an argument. We were on the way to her place after a movie and just before we got to your house, she threw her engagement ring from the pickup."

By now, two or three neighbors had gathered. Behind me, I heard one gasp. "Oh, dear."

I continued. "The ring is very valuable. It cost me almost five thousand dollars, and I'm still paying on it." I paused. "I'd sure appreciate it if you'd let me keep looking for it, ma'am."

At that moment, a slender man in a T-shirt and shorts came onto the porch and stopped at her side. "What's going on, Martha?"

"His fiancé threw her engagement ring from the car. He's trying to find it."

Cobb chuckled and descended the steps. "Well, we'll give you a hand, fella. Come on, Martha."

His willingness to help made me feel like a heel for what I had to do, but, if they hadn't lied, such a deception would not have been necessary. I turned to face him. "That won't be necessary, Mr. Cobb."

He jerked to a halt, staring at me in shock.

I hastened to explain. "I've been trying to get in touch with you, but your wife kept telling me you were out of town."

His slender face twisted in anger. He muttered a curse and took a step toward me.

I glanced over my shoulder, and in a soft voice the neighbors couldn't overhear, said, "I don't want trouble, Mr. Cobb, but it's me or the police."

That stopped him. The anger fled his face.

I continued in hushed tones. "Chief Ibbara gave me

the go-ahead to find out what happened to the Piri Reis Map. I know you've filed suit against Bernard Odom three times, and I also know you claim the map is yours. All I want to do is talk, nothing more." I handed him my PI license.

He studied it, then looked up at me, indecision filling his eyes. Finally, he sighed and nodded. "I don't have a choice, huh?"

I glanced at his wide-eyed wife who had her fists pressed against her lips in disbelief. I shrugged. "Not really."

The living room, while showing its age, was neat and orderly. Cobb pointed to a wingback chair at the end of a coffee table and he and his wife sat on the couch. "So? What is so important that you had to sneak around to find me?"

The hair on the back of my neck bristled but I held my tongue. "You know the Piri Reis is missing." Before he could respond, I continued. "Edna Hudson told you the other day when you called and wanted to stop by and visit with Ted." I smiled apologetically at Mrs. Cobb. "That's how I knew your wife was . . . Well, that's how I knew you weren't in Florida."

She looked around at him apologetically.

"I'm not going to blow smoke, Mr. Cobb. You claim the map is partially yours. That makes you a primary suspect in the theft." I paused. "And what happened up in Seattle twenty years ago doesn't help."

He and his wife looked at each other in alarm. He

laid his hand on hers. "We knew it might come up about the vase, Martha."

She closed her eyes and dropped her chin to her chest.

Cobb leaned back on the couch, crossing his arms over his chest. "So, what do you want to know?"

"Two or three things, really, but first, October second, say from eight to nine o'clock that night . . . Where were you?"

Without hesitation, he shot back. "Here. Martha and I were here all evening."

I glanced at Martha. She opened her eyes and looked at me. "I don't suppose anyone else saw you, Mr. Cobb?"

A faint grin curled one side of his lips. "No." I had a feeling he was lying.

At that moment the phone rang in another room. Martha excused herself.

After she left, I continued, "You were together all evening?"

Cobb leaned back on the couch. He hesitated. "No. After dinner at six-thirty, Martha went upstairs, and I went to my office to catch up on some bookwork."

I frowned. "How do you remember that? I mean, how do you remember what you did on that specific evening over two weeks ago?"

With a sly gleam in his eye, he replied, "Martha and I had talked about the exhibit at dinner."

His wife peered around the corner. "I'm sorry to interrupt, Leo, but Albert Cord is on the phone. He says it's urgent."

Cobb rose quickly. "This is important. I'll only be a minute."

I held up a hand to say "Go right ahead."

Mrs. Cobb returned and gingerly sat on the couch, folding her hands in her lap and giving me an uncomfortable smile. "Would you care for anything to drink, Mr. Boudreaux?"

I smiled warmly. "No, thank you, Mrs. Cobb." Back in Louisiana, there's an old saying that 'sometimes even a blind dog finds a bone.' Well, I was that blind dog. I couldn't believe my luck. I had the two of them apart for a few moments. Casually, I said, "So, you two spent the evening together on October second."

"Yes," she replied softly.

"Watching TV?"

She nodded. "Yes. All evening."

Either she was lying, or he was lying. Probably both. "So, there is no way he could have left the house without your knowing."

Mrs. Cobb stiffened. "No. Oh, no. Leo was home all night. I would have seen him if he'd left."

Cobb returned. He glanced at his wife, then sat on the couch. "A prospective client," he muttered.

"That's always good," I replied amiably. "Now, another question. You sued Odom three times. Can I ask why?"

His eyes blazed. "I don't mind telling you. That no good cheat and I worked together for several years. I found him some good deals, and then he started reneging on some of our agreements. We never put things down on paper." He grimaced. "I should have insisted but it was a handshake sort of thing. That's how I've always worked, and up until Bernard, I'd never had any problems. At first, there were none with him, but then he started backing out on some of our deals after I had obligated myself. I sued him twice for breach of contract. I won one, lost the other. Well, that must've got under his skin for he started spreading lies about me and my work in the art community." He paused. "If you know anything about the art community, it is a close-knit group of snobs. Word spreads fast. His lies cost me business. I sued him for slander, but he had political influence." He shrugged. "I lost that one."

"And that's when things started going bad for you financially?"

He frowned in surprise. "How did you know?"

"I know a lot. I know you filed for bankruptcy last year. Must be tough to spend thirty years building something only to see it torn down by lies."

Dropping his gaze to the coffee table, Cobb nodded emphatically. "Yeah."

"And I know you could lose this beautiful home."

Martha Cobb pressed her hand to her lips and looked at her husband in shock. "Leo!"

He shook his head in dismay. "We're not going to lose it, Martha. I got it worked out. I didn't tell you because I didn't want to worry you."

She just stared at him.

I continued. "What about the map? Why do you think it belongs to you? At least, part of it."

"That's why I sued him the first time. We agreed if I could find it, he'd buy it and my commission would be half interest in the map. He backed out. He paid me my standard ten percent commission, insisting we had never agreed on any partnership arrangement."

"How long ago was that?"

"Five years."

"Is that when you told him you'd get the map one way or another?"

Cobb's face crumbled. "How—how—"

"Ted Odom."

His wife looked up at him in alarm. "Leo. You didn't tell me that."

He shook his head impatiently. "It was just a figure of speech, Martha. Sure I wanted the map, but I did not steal it. And that's the truth." He turned back to me. "Well, any more questions?"

"Yeah, a couple more. Moffit at the museum said you offered him the map. Why would you do that if you and Odom were in it together?"

His face blanched. He stammered.

I had him on the ropes, so I threw another punch. "One more question. Why are you and your wife lying about the evening of October second?"

He glanced at his wife in surprise.

She shook her head. "I didn't tell him anything, Leo."

Cobb shot me a look of pure rage.

"Look, Mr. Cobb, either explain to me or the police why your wife claims you watched TV together all evening and you claim she went upstairs and you worked in your office."

The two just stared at me.

Finally, I said, "One of you is lying, maybe both, I don't know which, but to be honest, what you say about how Odom cheated you is motive big-time. That's exactly how the cops will look at it." I shrugged. "So tell me or tell them."

Martha Cobb's eyes pleaded with her husband. "Tell him the truth, Leo. Tell him what you told me. Maybe he can help."

The anxiety in her voice sent prickles up my arms. Maybe he can help? Help how?

Leo Cobb's face turned ashen. He sagged back down on the couch. "All right. Yeah, I was there."

His wife wrung her hands.

He shook his head slowly. "It just doesn't seem fair."

Chapter Thirteen

I almost felt sorry for the broken man staring up at me. I've seen enough in my life to wonder just how a word like "fair" ever made it into our vocabulary— probably as the illegitimate offspring of "deceitful" and "underhanded."

Staring blankly at the coffee table, Cobb nodded slowly. In a monotone, he said, "I went there that night to steal the map. A wealthy industrial CEO in France wanted it for his private collection. Eight million dollars. I knew Bernard planned to attend the exhibition at the museum. Edna would be gone, and I figured Teddy would be out prowling the streets like he always is. There was a light on in Bernard's office. That didn't surprise me. He often left his lights burning all night."

He paused and drew a deep breath. "The foyer light was on. I unlocked the door and went inside. I figured if he was in his office, I'd come up with some excuse."

He hesitated when he saw the sudden frown on my face. "Oh, I had a key. That's how close Bernard and I were. We'd worked together so often that I would come and go as needed. Anyway, when I opened the door to his office, I saw him on the floor. At first, I thought he had fallen and knocked himself out. I tried to rouse him but he didn't respond. I put my ear to his chest but there was no heartbeat."

He hesitated and shivered. "It was horrible. There was a bloody knot on his head, and his eyes were open. I'll never forget the look in those bloodshot eyes of his. It was like he was staring at me, accusing me."

His voice choked off, and he sat staring at the coffee table. His wife scooted to his side and draped her arm over his shoulders to console him.

After a moment, Cobb looked up at me, his face haggard. "Yeah, I was going to steal the map, but when I found him like that, I ran. As fast as I could, I ran from that house."

"Why didn't you call the police?"

The older couple looked at each other desperately. In a cracked voice, he replied, "In our last argument, I threatened to kill Bernard. His secretary heard me."

"Edna Hudson?"

"Yes," he replied almost inaudibly.

In a soft voice, I asked, "About what time were you there?"

"Around nine-thirty or thereabouts." He looked up,

his eyes pleading for understanding. "I didn't know what had happened to him. From the knot on his head, I figured someone hit him. I was scared. Like I said, I couldn't afford to be involved. Edna knew I had threatened him. I knew I would be the main suspect."

He paused. "Later, I kept waiting for the police to show up. I knew Edna would tell them of my threat, and then I read it was an accident." He forced a weak smile. "You've no idea how relieved I was." He paused and frowned. "To be honest, I really thought someone had killed Bernard."

I remained silent.

He shook his head. "I still don't know why Edna didn't say something about it to the cops."

His last remark made me wonder the same thing. Why hadn't Edna mentioned Cobb's threat? I filed it away in the back of my head. "You say you went there to steal the map. Did you know where the map was?"

"No."

"So you were just going to tear the office apart?"

Cobb hesitated. His eyes narrowed shrewdly, then opened wide. He drew a deep breath. "No. The truth is, I had forgotten all about a sarcastic comment he had made during one of our arguments. Then one day last month, for whatever reason, I remembered that remark." He studied me a moment before continuing. "I wasn't going to mention it. Not to you or anyone, but I'm tired of all the hassle, of the suspicion."

I waited expectantly. When he didn't continue I started to prompt him, but his wife did it for me. "What did he say, Leo? If it'll clear you of any suspicion, tell Mr. Boudreaux."

He looked around at her. His eyes grew soft, and a gentle smile played over his lips. "All right, Martha. All right." He turned back to me. "About three, maybe four years ago, I told Bernard that one way or another, the Piri Reis would be mine. He laughed and pointed to those two printings on the den wall between the bookcases. Have you seen them?"

"The ones with a bunch of scribblings? Yeah."

"He said, you'll have to deal with those first."

I frowned. "Any idea what he meant?"

"No. I studied them, but I wasn't familiar with the writing. Bernard said they were from an obscure dynasty back around 3400 AD, so, I figured he meant the map was hidden behind one of them. They're all large enough." Cobb shook his head.

With a wry chuckle, I said, "I took both of those abstracts apart, down to the glass. There was no map there."

His shoulders sagged. He laughed bitterly. "Wouldn't you know? Even now, Bernard is getting the last laugh."

I studied him for a few moments. I wanted to believe the guy. From what I had seen, he was not clever enough to have feigned the whole interview. "You said you thought someone had murdered him."

Cobb nodded.

"Can you think of anyone who might have killed him?"

After a moment, he shook his head. "No, no one in

our circle, the art community, unless it was an accident. But on the other hand, I figure everyone who knew him believes he got what he deserved."

An accident! That was an interesting theory, although it had nothing to do with the map. "You mean, an argument or something, and someone pushed Odom?"

"Yeah, but . . . now that I think about it, I can tell you someone who wanted him dead. That niece of his."

Martha looked up in alarm at her husband, but he continued. "She was bleeding him dry. She was always wild, from the day Bernard first took her in. She was around fifteen or sixteen then. He put her in a private school, and then when she finished college she took off for Europe. She's back now, and from gossip I hear, she's wanting more money."

As I drove away from the Cobb home, I realized I was not much closer to finding the Piri Reis than when I first started. Still, I had two more suspects to interview—Lamia Sue Odom and Father Bertoldo Poggioreale.

Winding through the traffic, I replayed the last few days. I hadn't met one person yet who couldn't have taken the map. True, four or five had no motive, at least no obvious motive. The map belonged to Ted; Edna had a nice inheritance as did Lamia Sue, the niece I was on the way to see. They had no reason to steal it.

Hogg had been at the Odom mansion, but claimed he'd never gotten out of the Cadillac, which appeared to be true, for Edna had been in the house until seven when she'd left, and spotted the vehicle pulling away from the curb. Had he gone into the house, she would have seen him.

Cobb admitted being inside, in the den with the dead man. Had he stolen the map, he never would have admitted it. Thinking back over our interview, I knew Cobb just wasn't that clever of a liar.

Now, all I had to do was find out about Odom's niece and the good Father.

I've always enjoyed the San Antonio River Walk. To a Louisiana country boy, the exotic venue is as close to Venice as I'll ever get. Broad flagstone walks butting up against twelve-foot limestone walls line the twisting river. Large mosaics of striking artistic skill depicting the rich history of the Hispanic culture are set in the white limestone, reminding me of the ornate stained glass windows in churches back home. Sidewalk tables offer the opportunity to relax and watch the world saunter past.

From my inn, the Grand Isle, the Elena Towers was just a short stroll. The day was growing late. I had no idea if I could catch Lamia Sue Odom in or not, but I thought I'd give it a shot. If I didn't, I'd try again in the morning.

I had no sooner stepped onto the River Walk when I heard my name called. I looked around to see Jack Edney waving exuberantly from the other side of the river. "You coming over?" he shouted.

I nodded, irritated, then chided myself for being so.

Jack was a good friend, even if he could be a pest at times. Besides, after a visit with Lamia Sue, I wouldn't mind relaxing at one of the sidewalk tables with a drink and watching the world go by.

"How about something to drink?" he asked, grabbing my hand and pumping my arm like we hadn't seen each other in months.

"Not right now." I nodded to the Elena Towers in the next block. "I'm going to try to catch someone up there. Let's walk on down and get a table. You can enjoy one or two cool libations while I take care of some business."

"Sounds like a winner to me," he gushed.

Despite the tourist season being over and a slight nip in the air, there were still dozens of people on the walk. "So, what have you been up to?" I asked as we wound our way through the crowd.

"Not much. Went sightseeing after I got over my hangover." He laughed. "I still don't know how much I had to drink."

I laughed and patted his bulging belly, which was hard as a rock. "Enough, my friend. Enough."

"Anyway, I went to the Alamo. You know what that is, don't you?"

"Naturally. I might be from Louisiana but I've heard about the Alamo." I grinned to myself and needled him. "That's all I hear some of you Texans talk about, the Alamo. Wasn't that some saloon or gas station or something?"

"Best watch it, partner. Them's fighting words," he

replied with a grin. "Anyway, after the Alamo, I visited all of the missions. There are five of them. Did you know that? They were really interesting. I think I might take Diane to them."

I glanced at him. "She's coming down?"

"Later." He paused and grinned shyly at me. "We're thinking about getting married."

All I could do was gape at him. Finally, I found my voice. "Married? That's great, Jack. Great."

He looked deep into my eyes. "You sure, Tony? Really sure? After all, you and Diane were married."

I laughed. "Yeah, but you'll be a better man for her than I was."

He beamed. "I'm glad you think so." Jack continued to babble. I let it go in one ear and out the other, preferring the ambiance of the lazy river to the nightmares he was facing. As we passed beneath the Houston Street Bridge, I noticed five or six stylishly dressed men and women clustered against the rear wall at the back of the sidewalk. Behind them, a twelve-foot mosaic depicted a robed priest blessing a band of kneeling Indians.

One of the young men in the group glanced around surreptitiously before quickly handing a bill to a young brunet wearing heels, hip huggers, and one of those peasant blouses with a tie neck. Moments later, the group broke up. Two couples headed down the River Walk. And the young woman in heels, accompanied by a long-haired young woman in ripped jeans, western shirt, and sandals, headed upriver.

I chuckled softly. When I taught English in a high

school where administrators didn't want you to teach, parents were offended when you did, and students couldn't believe they were expected to learn, drugs were rampant. Obviously, they still were.

And the schools, for the most part, looked the other way. Oh, the schools made public gestures, media announcements, and ominous threats as to the dire consequences if a student were caught, but nine times out of ten, when an infraction occurred, strangely enough the circumstances usually faded into the night.

More than once, students in my English classes laughed and told me they could get me anything I wanted during the next break between classes. I never had the guts to take them up on it.

So, witnessing drug deals was nothing to get excited about, though in my twisted sense of perspective I could see the wry irony in a drug deal going down in front of a mosaic with a priest giving God's blessing to illiterate Indians. I glanced down at Jack, who was still babbling about his upcoming marriage.

At the Elena Towers, we found a table against the white limestone wall at the back of the sidewalk. Jack ordered a drink while I went inside. Lamia Sue Odom was in room 718. There was no answer. I glanced at my watch: 5:40.

I stopped at the desk and left a message including my cell number and the fact I would be on the sidewalk outside the Elena Towers until six thirty. She could identify me by my tweed jacket.

Outside, the sun was dropping behind skyscrapers,

casting shadows across the River Walk. I joined Jack and ordered a cool rum mai tai.

"That was fast," he said.

"She wasn't in. I left word for her to meet us here."

I had no idea what kind of surprise I was in for.

About thirty minutes later, the two young women I had spotted under the bridge sashayed past, heading up the stairs into the Elena Towers.

Frowning, I glanced over my shoulder as they disappeared inside. I felt the hair on the back of my neck bristle. Surely not.

Five minutes later, the one in heels and hip huggers appeared at our table. Her dark brown hair framed her heart-shaped face attractively. "Excuse me, were you looking for me?"

I gaped at her for a moment, then glanced past her, at her friend in the ripped jeans. "Are you Lamia Sue Odom?"

She smiled brightly at Jack and then back at me. "Yes. Who are you?"

Chapter Fourteen

Rising, I introduced Jack and myself.

Frowning, she said, "Boudreaux? Have we ever met?"

"No. Your cousin, Ted, hired me."

Her face lit in understanding. "Oh, yes. You're the private investigator who is going to find Uncle Bernard's map." She nodded emphatically. "Ted told me about you."

I gestured to an empty chair. "I'd like to visit with you for a few minutes—if you have the time."

She glanced at Jack, then back at me. "Certainly. I can't stay long. My roommate and I have an appointment in thirty minutes." She slipped in at the table and ordered a Perrier with a slice of lime.

And I'll bet I know what kind of appointment, I told myself. "This won't take long, Miss Odom. I'm just trying to pick a few brains. See what I can find out about the map."

Jack pushed to his feet. "You want me to leave, Tony?" He glanced at Lamia Sue.

She spoke up. "Heavens no." She looked me straight in the eyes. "I've got nothing to hide about anything."

I continued. "The map. Have you ever seen it?"

"No. Uncle Bernard purchased it while I was in Spain. He put it away for safekeeping."

"Your cousin thinks someone murdered your uncle and then stole the map."

Shaking her head slowly, she laughed harshly. "Ted's always been suspicious like that. He's paranoid, always worrying about things and sticking his nose where it doesn't belong. All I know is that Uncle Bernard hid the map somewhere in the den. At least that's what he told me." Her hostility toward her cousin was obvious.

"Do you think someone might have killed your uncle?"

"No. It was an accident. Uncle Bernard wasn't paying attention to where he was walking and tripped. He hit his head." She shrugged. "That's all there was to it."

"Do you mind telling me where you were that night?"

A bright smile popped on her lips and her eyes glittered with amusement. "Am I a suspect, or something?"

"Nope." I shook my head and lied. "Not really. You have a big inheritance coming. I don't see what you would have to gain by taking the map."

She smiled up at me mischievously. "Well, you might be wise to make me a suspect." I frowned. "To tell the truth, Mr. Boudreaux, I don't know. Some friends and I partied that night out at Lake Travis. I don't remember too much about it except I woke up in this yacht the next morning about ten." She stared at me, a hint of amusement flashing in her dark eyes.

At least she was honest. "Whose place was it? Remember?"

She laughed. "I wasn't that zonked, Horace Shackleford. You know, Shackleford Mall."

I couldn't resist a grin. If she got herself zonked, she got zonked with good company. Shackleford was known as Mall Master of Texas, even up in Dallas, which fancied itself as the Paris of the Southwest. "What about Leo Cobb or Joe Hogg? Ever hear those names?"

"No." She shrugged sheepishly. "I really didn't know any of Uncle Bernard's acquaintances. I'm sorry I can't be any more help but I never paid any attention to my uncle's business." She paused, and in a sarcastic tone, added, "I leave all of that up to Cousin Ted."

"Trouble between you two?"

Lamia shook her head. "Not really. He's just a wimpy little boy who never grew up."

Jack ordered us another round of drinks as I watched her walk away, remembering Patsy Fusco's observation about her.

Jack sipped his old fashioned. "She any help?"

I pondered his question seriously. In the past, I'd bounced ideas off Jack. Sometimes, he'd responded with ideas I'd never considered. "Not really. I've got one more person to talk to. The problem is there are several who would have probably stolen the map if they had known where it was."

Jack interrupted. "Huh? What do you mean, if they knew where it was?"

"Supposedly, the old man hid the map. Now, his son can't find it, so he thinks it was stolen."

He frowned. "Doesn't he know where his old man hid it?"

"No."

He looked at me in disbelief. "You gotta be kidding. He doesn't know where his old man hid it, so now he thinks it's stolen? That's kinda screwy."

I waved him off. "It's a long story. Anyway, there's only a couple of individuals who would really profit by the map, but at the same time, they couldn't offer it on the market because the map is so well-known that its sale would be impossible to keep secret."

"Well-known? I never heard of it."

I chuckled. "I mean in the art community."

Jack drained the last of his old fashioned and pushed to his feet. "Forget about it all. Let's go get us something to eat. Next to my hotel is a place called Elizio's. Supposed to serve great quesadillas with garlic shrimp, roasted pepper, and goat cheese."

I chuckled. "Why not?"

By the time we reached Elizio's, the sun had set. The quesadillas were delicious although an extra shot or two of tequila in the recipe would have added an extra zest to the dish. Halfway through the meal, my cell rang. It was Janice, wondering if I was coming back to Austin over the weekend.

"I wish I could but things are going pretty slow. I need to hang around here and keep working so I can get back to our Halloween dance next Saturday."

"I'll miss you," she replied wistfully.

I held my breath but she didn't continue. "I'll miss you. By the way, how's your aunt?"

"Much better. She's up and around. Not quite her old self but doing very well."

"Then I tell you what. Why don't you hop in that new little Jaguar roadster and buzz down here Saturday afternoon? We'll have a romantic dinner on the River Walk and take in the Bracero Festival at my hotel Saturday night. I'll even get you a room if you want one."

She hesitated. "What time?"

"Noon at the Grand Isle. You know it?"

"I'll be there. And Tony?"

"Yeah?"

In a sultry voice, she added, "Forget the extra room."

After punching off, instead of popping my cell in my pocket, I laid it on the table and grabbed my drink. Saturday had just become a very important day for me.

After another drink, I said good night and headed across the river to my hotel. Jack remained behind, ordering one more old fashioned.

* * *

When I opened the door to my room and stepped inside, a hand seized my arm and jerked me into the room. I fought for balance, and when I steadied myself, I was looking into the cold muzzle of a snub-nosed revolver. Behind it was a man dressed in black and wearing a ski mask.

I held up my hands. "Take what you want, pal. You won't get any argument from me."

He snorted. "I don't want nothing from you, Boudreaux. It's time for you get out of San Antone. This town ain't healthy for you, and I'm here to show you how sick it can make you."

At that moment, Jack appeared in the open door. "Hey, what's going on? Tony? You all right?"

The thug jerked around. "What the—"

I leaped, smashing into his back and driving him through the open door and slamming him into a startled Jack Edney. The three of us bounced off the wall and fell in a snarl of arms and legs.

By the time we untangled ourselves, the goon had vanished down the hall and out a rear exit. Jack and I sat on the floor looking at each other.

He shook his head. "What was all that about?"

At that moment, the door across the hall opened, and an irate man stuck his head out. "What's all the racket out here? We're trying to sleep."

I held up my hand. "Sorry. I tripped over my own feet and knocked my friend down."

His lips curled in a sneer. "Bunch of drunks," he muttered. He slammed the door, and I heard him shout,

"I told you we shouldn't come here, Myrtle. This whole town is full of sin and transgressions."

Back in my room, Jack handed me my cell phone. "You left this on the table. I was bringing it to you. Looks like I got here just in time. Are you sure you're all right, Tony? That mug had a gun."

"Yeah, I'm fine." I gestured to a chair in front of the curtained sliding doors that opened onto the tiny balcony outside my second-floor room. I plopped down on the bed and stared at Jack. "But I can't figure what's going on."

Jack frowned. He tried to lean forward, but his enormous belly prevented it. "You mean, this wasn't the first time something's happened."

I nodded slowly. "Yeah. Last Tuesday on the way down from Austin, an eighteen-wheeler ran me off the road. Then that night, my room—well, you were with me. You remember what it looked like. Someone had torn it apart."

He looked at me blankly. "When?"

"Tuesday night. When you got snockered."

A sheepish grin curled his lips. "Jeez, Tony, I'm sorry. All I remember is waking up in here. I just figured you'd thrown the mattress on the floor for me."

I groaned. "Anyway, the next day, someone planted a bindle of coke in my truck, and now this."

He leaned back and folded his arms over the top of his belly. "I'd say someone doesn't want you to find that map, old friend."

A soft chuckle rolled up from my throat. "That's what puzzles me. Why would someone not want me to find the map? The only answer I see is that whoever wants me off the case knows the location of the map and has a buyer."

The concern on Jack's face deepened. "Listen, you want me to spend the night here? I don't mind, you know."

If I were into kissing men, I would have kissed Jack then. "No, thanks. I'll be fine."

He pushed to his feet. "How about breakfast in the morning at Pooky's?"

"All right, but I'm getting an early start. Seven o'clock?"

"See you then."

After Jack left, I locked the door, flipped on the TV and lay back on the bed, trying to sort the confused thoughts tumbling through my head.

The niece, Lamia Sue Odom, had found herself a somewhat profitable but highly unstable business in dealing. She appeared to be a bright young woman, which made her activities all that much more puzzling.

She was a small operator, probably one of the reasons she was still alive. The life of a drug dealer is usually measured in months, not years.

I glanced at the clock. Almost ten. Edna would be gone. I made a mental note to visit her the next day. In the morning, I would pay a visit to Father Bertoldo Poggioreale out at L'Università di Grazia e la Fratellanza, the University of Grace and Brotherhood.

After a quick shower, I plopped into bed just in time to join a late-night program of *Forensic Secrets* on TV. The program was an anthology of autopsies on various means of death: gunshot, strangulation, stabbing, clubbing, poison, and electrocution.

Somewhere between poison and electrocution, I began dozing. I turned off the TV and dropped into a dreamless sleep.

In the early morning hours, my eyes popped open, and I stared at the ceiling above my head, a remark from the TV program sticking in my head.

"No way," I muttered, jumping out of bed and stumping my toe on the nightstand. Amid a few sincere curses, I hopped to the table and flipped on the lamp. I fumbled for my note cards, hastily shuffling through them and muttering to myself.

I hesitated, reminding myself I was venturing into a forbidden aspect of the case, namely Bernard Odom's death. According to both Teddy and Chief Ibbara, the JP ruled it accidental.

I was asking for trouble if I stuck my nose in, but if my idea was right, that would explain the attempts to run me off the case. On top of that, it might mean that Bernard Julius Odom's death was not accidental.

Chapter Fifteen

Finally, I found the card for which I was searching.
I read Cobb's words aloud.

*"It was horrible. There was a bloody knot on his
head, and his eyes were open. I'll never forget the
look in those bloodshot eyes of his. It was like he
was staring at me, accusing me."*

Bloodshot eyes!

I reached for my laptop. As I booted up, I remembered the distinctive characteristics that suggested strangulation and suffocation from the TV program.

In strangulation, there are marks obvious to the naked
eye on the neck: bruises, fingernail imprints, or ligature
marks. Obvious evidence suggesting suffocation would
be hemorrhages in the eyes, face, lungs, and neck area.

Could that be the explanation for the bloodshot eyes Cobb witnessed?

As soon as my homepage flashed on the screen, I pulled up a search engine and inputted *physical evidence suffocation.* I quickly discovered that I might have been jumping to conclusions.

According to one source, any hemorrhaging that suggests suffocation is usually characterized by red dots the size of a pin's head, usually in the eyes, face, and neck areas. Bloodshot eyes could simply result from dehydration after death.

I reread the description, noting the qualifying words, *usually* and *could.*

I leaned back in my chair and stared at the laptop. But what if that *usually* or *could* did not apply in this situation? If Odom was murdered, it was around nine o'clock, give or take thirty minutes. The killer had to be someone he knew for there was no sign of struggle, only the overturned coffee table. Someone could have struck him on the back of his head, so that he fell forward, his forehead striking the coffee table. When his assailant saw he wasn't dead, he suffocated him.

It was a neat little theory. And no way to prove it, especially since the local fount of wisdom known as the justice of the peace declared the death accidental, thus eliminating any further forensic investigation.

The second little problem was the map. Over the last few years, I had become fairly expert in body language, and unless those I had interviewed were accomplished liars, no one had discovered the map. So, why would someone kill Odom without learning the location of the Piri Reis? Obviously, I told myself, the killer thought he knew the location.

And now the efforts to run me off made sense. Murder would be reason enough for the killer to fear my snooping might expose him. But, I reminded myself ruefully, how do you prove it?

Suddenly, a flash of inspiration hit me. It doesn't happen often but this time it was brilliant. They might not have autopsied Bernard Odom then, but there was no reason Ted Odom couldn't insist on exhuming his father's body and performing one.

Excited, I reached for the phone. My eyes fell on the clock. Almost four. Suddenly I was exhausted. My eyes burned from lack of sleep. I could take care of everything in the morning. I booted off the laptop, flipped off the lights, and climbed back into bed, but not before I called the desk for a six o'clock wake-up call.

Jack was waiting for me at Pooky's. He had no plans for the day. "Loaf around. Watch the women pass. You know, all that important stuff." He paused. "Unless you wouldn't mind me riding along with you today."

"Come on, Jack. Remember Bayou Teche?"

"Yeah, and the loup garou. Who could forget that?"

"It'll be the same thing. I'm going out to some university, then out to San Madreas. You'd be sitting in the truck."

"Fine with me, but let's go in my Caddie. I'll sit in

the air conditioning and drink beer while you're doing all your private investigating stuff."

I cautioned him. "Remember. No beer while we're driving."

He held up his hand. "Hey, would I do something like that? That's against the law."

I snorted. "Since when did something like breaking the law stop Jack Edney?"

He roared with laughter. "Don't worry, Tony. I'll be a good little boy. I'll pick you up in front of the hotel. Fifteen minutes."

Up in my room, I called the mansion. No answer, so I left word on Ted's voice mail that I'd see him around ten.

I wanted to visit with him about the exhumation and then spend a few minutes picking Edna's brain. I was curious as to what kind of financial support Odom had arranged for Lamia Sue throughout her years in Europe.

An unpleasant thought had popped into my head that the young woman might have herself so far in hock to her supplier that she had to take extreme measures to cover herself, those measures including the Piri Reis. If that were true, then she must have known the location of the map despite her assertions otherwise.

To my surprise, Jack pulled up to the curb in the same Cadillac we had driven to Bayou Teche the previous spring, an XLR with the 4.6L V-8 engine and five-speed automatic. Usually, he bought a new one every three months.

"I'm puzzled," I remarked after closing the door and buckling up.

He frowned. "At what?"

"Same Caddie." I laughed. "I figured Diane would have talked you into a new one by now."

He flexed his fingers about the wheel. "If she had her way, I would." He paused. "Tell me, Tony. When you two were together, did she spend like she does now?"

I chuckled. "No idea. We didn't have the money to spend."

He grunted. "Like I said, we've talked about marriage but the way she goes through money makes me wonder."

The grounds of the University of Grace and Brotherhood sprawled over about forty acres in the middle of a bustling commercial community twelve to fifteen miles south of downtown San Antonio. Constructed of white limestone from the surrounding quarries, the administration building perched on the crest of a hill. In a circle about the ad building were eight or ten similarly constructed buildings housing various educational disciplines. At the base of the gentle rise were half a dozen dormitories.

At first glance, it was obvious the university enjoyed the beneficence of generous endowments. Curving sidewalks lined with myriad flowers and shrubs crisscrossed the lush lawn. Small gazebos dotted the campus, and occasional fishponds offered moments of serenity for the students. And no football stadium.

Father Bertoldo Poggioreale was a tenured professor in the Department of History, in the Blythe Building.

His first class, European Medieval History, began at eight on Mondays, Wednesdays, and Fridays. I arrived at the end of that class.

After his students left, I stepped into the classroom, which was bright and airy, hardly the atmosphere in which you would expect a drudgingly boring medieval history class to be taught.

Father Poggioreale was seated behind his desk, catching up on paperwork. I knew he was fifty-five, but his black wavy hair, olive complexion and taut skin cut twenty years off his appearance.

He smiled warmly when he spotted me. "Yes, sir. Can I help you?"

"If you're Father Poggioreale, you can."

His smile grew wider. "Then I can."

I introduced myself. By now, students were drifting in for the next class. "I'd like to find some time to visit with you about the Piri Reis Map. I understand you are an expert on ancient maps. And if my sources are correct, you were a student under the seismologist Reverend William Chanlin, whom the Naval Hydrographic Office took to Antarctica to validate the map."

His broad forehead furrowed. "Ah, the Piri Reis. I read about Mr. Odom. Such a shame."

More students filled the room. "Is there some time

today when we could visit? I think your expertise might prove very helpful."

His frown deepened. "I don't understand. How?"

"The Piri Reis has disappeared. I was wondering—"

"You were wondering if I took it?"

Chapter Sixteen

H is candor surprised me. Something about the good father didn't ring true but it was as nebulous as a puff of smoke. "No. The truth is I'm looking for leads on the map. I figured with your contacts, you might have some ideas."

He smiled brightly. "Wait just a few minutes. This is exam day for this class. An essay on Medieval Ethics under the reign of Henry VIII We'll have forty-five minutes. We can talk here." He indicated a chair at the side of the room. "If you wish, you can sit over there until I get the class started."

A few of the twenty-odd students glanced curiously at me. I studied Father Poggioreale as he spoke with the students, but when he gave them their test assignment they all turned assiduously to the task.

After instructing the students on the exam, he pulled

a chair up beside me where he could also watch the class. Eagerly, he said, "Now, Mr. Boudreaux. What can I tell you?"

He seemed too willing to help me. Or he might just be one of those rare souls who are always ready to offer assistance to anyone.

"Being an expert, and with all your contacts, can you think of anyone so, ah, so—"

"Covetous?"

I grinned. "As good a word as any. So covetous as to steal the map?"

With a slight shrug of his shoulders, he replied, "No. Sorry. My life, as you can see, is fairly cloistered." He nodded to the campus beyond the windows. "The university and all."

At risk of my being labeled a cynic, the good father seemed a little too noble for me. "Well, can I ask why you wanted to buy it?"

My question caught him off guard, and for a moment he hesitated. Then, regaining his composure, he replied with smug assurance. "I knew the value of the map but the dean said the university could not afford such a price. I kept hoping Mr. Odom would reduce the price to the point we could bring the map to the university. It would have been a magnificent addition to our collection of various medieval artifacts. The map was drawn in 1519, you know."

I frowned. "I thought it was 1513?"

He hesitated, then grinned sheepishly as a touch of

color rose in his cheeks. "You're right, of course. I was thinking of another map—1513."

"You must have really wanted it bad to try three times to buy it."

"Nothing is more important than educating these students." He nodded to the sea of bent heads in the classroom.

"I understand that. I taught English up in Austin several years ago."

He arched an eyebrow. "Oh, why'd you leave?"

I chuckled. "Just say I didn't have your dedication."

A self-satisfied smile played over his lips, and a little too nobly, he replied, "It is a calling."

"Did you know Bernard Odom?"

"Yes, but not well. From time to time, he inquired of the authenticity of various maps he was considering for his collection, but for the most part it was a business relationship."

"One more question, Father, and then I'm finished. The night of October second. Do you remember where you were?"

"What day was that?"

"A Monday."

"Ah. Mondays and Wednesday nights I have a seven-to-ten class on religious ethics." He paused and nodded to a young man in the end seat on the front row. "In fact, Jeremy there is in that class. You can ask him if you wish."

I shook my head, noting that the young student wore

white shorts and a red T-shirt. "No. I'm satisfied." I rose and offered my hand. "Thanks, Father. I appreciate it."

Jack had parked in the shade of several ancient elms near the history building. While I had been inside, he'd lowered the top on his convertible. He reached to start the car when I climbed in. "Not yet," I said. "I want to talk to a student." Father Poggioreale had been very open and candid. Still, something nagged at me about the man, something I couldn't pin down.

Maybe I had been around Al Grogan too much and his suspicious nature was rubbing off on me. Poggioreale was probably just what he seemed, a conscientious teacher concerned with nothing more than helping his students. Still, I wanted to visit with two individuals— the young student, Jeremy, and the dean of the History Department.

I glanced at my watch. I wasn't going to make my ten o'clock appointment with Ted and Edna. I called to inform her but I only got voice mail. I left a message.

Ten minutes later, students emerged from the history complex. I spotted an animated young man in white shorts and a red T-shirt strolling with two other young men.

I watched as they crossed the street and ducked into Bucky's Burgers. "Back in a minute," I told Jack, climbing from the car.

"Now where?"

"That hamburger joint over there."

His face brightened. "Hey, bring me back a couple, okay? Everything on them."

I rolled my eyes. Breakfast at seven, and now three hours later, two hamburgers all the way. Jack Edney was the proverbial hollow leg.

Laughing students packed Bucky's. Steam filled the kitchen in the back as plate after plate of hamburgers, tacos, hot dogs, and half a dozen other high-fat, high-cholesterol entrees—all with French fries and served by liberal arts graduates—slid across the counter. And I thought Cajuns' four food groups of fried fish, fried shrimp, fried crawfish, and a sixpack had a lock on clogging arteries. Bucky's menu would run them a close race.

I spotted Jeremy and his two friends on stools at the end of the counter.

Without looking at him, I sidled up beside Jeremy and ordered two hamburgers to go.

He glanced up at me. "Hi."

I looked around.

An infectious grin played over his lips. "You're the guy that was in Papa Poggy's classroom last period."

"Papa Poggy?" I frowned.

One of his friends laughed good-naturedly. "Yeah, Father Bertoldo Poggioreale, better known as Papa Poggy."

I laughed with them, remembering my college days and the fun we had baiting professors. "Yeah, we were talking about maps."

Jeremy groaned. "That's Papa Poggy's obsession, maps. But he's a good teacher. I like him. All of his classes are real interesting. Makes history come alive, you know?"

"Yeah," the other two joined in.

"Is that all he teaches, history?"

At that moment, the waitress slid their hamburgers and drinks on the counter before them.

While Jeremy opened his hamburger to dump catsup on it, he continued. "Nope. Monday and Wednesday nights, he teaches a class on religious ethics." With his hamburger, he gestured to his friends. "We're in it, just the three of us. It's a neat class."

Both cheeks bulging with hamburger, one of the boys managed to laugh. "Yeah, and sometimes, it is just the three of us."

The other two chuckled.

"Oh?"

Jeremy swallowed a mouthful that would choke a horse. "Yeah. Sometimes Papa Poggy comes in, checks roll, and gives us our work, then goes to his office. He always gets back before class is over."

I told myself I'd just found a bird nest on the ground. "He probably has a lot of trust in you boys."

"We have an honor code here. No one breaks it."

I glanced at the other two boys. They nodded.

"Well," I said casually, fishing for more information, "that gives him time to catch up on some paperwork."

One of the boys snickered. "I wouldn't call it paperwork."

Jeremy snapped. "Come on, Georgie. We don't know that for sure. Give the guy a break."

"Yeah, we do."

"No, we don't."

In their lighthearted squabble, they momentarily forgot about me.

Georgie elbowed the young man between them. "What about it, Freddy?"

Freddy shook his head. "I'm not sure what he's doing, Jeremy. You know yourself, this last month he's left as soon as he checks roll, and doesn't get back until just before class is over. I know for a fact Papa Poggy hasn't been in his office this last month. His light's on but he isn't there. I've looked when I went to the john."

"He could be somewhere else in the building," Jeremy protested.

"Yeah," Georgie responded with a sneer, "and I'm an alien from outer space." He snorted. "I don't know what he's doing when he's gone but he always comes back looking awfully happy."

The waitress handed me my bag of burgers. I nodded to the boys. "Take care. Nice talking to you."

Now, all I had to do was talk to the dean.

Chapter Seventeen

I slid into the Cadillac and handed Jack his burgers.

"Ready to go?"

"Not yet." I nodded to the Blythe Building. "I need to mull a couple of things over first."

"Whatever." Jack unwrapped a burger and popped a Budweiser beer.

I stared blankly at the Blythe Building, trying to gather the thoughts bouncing off the insides of my head.

First, I learned that Papa Poggy had probably been out of his classroom on the second of October. And according to young Freddy, he wasn't in his office. That meant on the second, he could have been at the Odom mansion. A stretch, I knew, but a possibility.

Second, no instructor, tenured or otherwise, could purchase any item for the university without the approval of his dean, and then the acquisition involved purchase orders that were in turn approved by the business manager. So, all I had to do was find out if Poggioreale had spoken with his dean about the Piri Reis. If the History Department was indeed interested in the map then I'd forget about Papa Poggy, but if they had no knowledge then that put an entirely different complexion on the good father.

From Information, I got the number of the dean of the History Department on the campus.

"I'm sorry," a young woman said. "Dean Coggins is out the rest of the day. He'll be back Monday. Would you care to leave a message?"

"If you don't mind." I gave her my name and hotel. "If I'm not in he can leave a number."

"May I ask what this is in reference to?"

"Certainly. I wanted to talk to the dean about donations to his department." If I'd ever known of a surefire trick to get an educational professional to call back, it was by suggesting they might receive a donation.

When I punched off, Jack said, "Ready to go?"

I frowned at him. He'd polished off two hamburgers and a beer in five minutes. I just shook my head. I lost count of the times I'd fussed at Jack about scarfing his food down. He always patted his belly and laughed. "Cast-iron stomach, Tony. That's the secret."

"You bet. Okay, I'm ready."

"Where to?"

"2112 Fairchild. In San Madreas."

Jack whistled softly when we pulled up beside the mansion. "Hey, this is something else. I wouldn't mind a shack like this. You think they'd let me see the place?"

I figured Edna could show him around while Ted and I spoke. Then Ted could take over while I visited with Edna. "I don't see why not."

We climbed the steps to the sprawling porch and rang the bell. Jack nodded at the frosted glass in the upper half of the door. "That looks like the real thing."

Moments later, the door swung open. Ted grinned. "You didn't have to knock."

"Habit," I replied, introducing Jack. "He admires your house. Maybe Edna can show him around while you and I visit."

He gave me a puzzled look, then replied, "She's out this morning. She'll be in after one or so." He smiled at Jack. "Mr. Edney, you're welcome to look through the house. There's a maid around here somewhere. If she asks anything, tell her I said it was okay." He pointed to the southern corner of the floor. "We'll be in the den when you finish."

Ted led the way into the den. My eyes went instinctively to the rich Oriental carpet between the end table and coffee table where Bernard Odom had fallen. Ted closed the door behind us and motioned to the couch.

He sat and scooted around to face me. "I haven't

seen you for the last couple of days. How are things going?"

I held out my hand and fluttered it from side to side.

"Hard to say. But what I really wanted to talk about was your father."

"Father?"

"Yes. There was no autopsy."

He shrugged. "So?"

"Look, I'll explain later, but how would you feel about exhuming your father's body for an autopsy?"

A frown erased the puzzlement on his face. "Impossible."

I leaned forward, my voice earnest. "But why?"

A faint grin curled his lips. "Father was cremated."

I couldn't have been any more stunned than if my Significant Other's seventy-five-year-old Aunt Beatrice had strolled in au naturel. I stammered for words but none would form.

Ted nodded. "That's what he wanted. I thought I mentioned it to you." His brow furrowed. "You seem upset. Why? What would an autopsy prove?"

I closed my eyes and muttered curses. Finally, I drew a deep breath and looked at Ted. "At first when you told me about the case, you said you thought your father had been murdered."

"Yes." He nodded. "I just don't think Father fell over the ottoman."

"What do you think happened?"

He pursed his lips and drew a deep breath. He released it quickly and said, "I think someone wanted the map and struck father on the head." He paused and studied me curiously. "What do you think?"

I considered his question. "I think there is the possibility he might have been murdered but I don't think a blow to the back of the head killed him."

He leaned forward. "What then?"

Nodding to the throw pillow behind him, I replied, "That."

"Huh?" He held up the pillow. "I don't understand."

"An autopsy would have helped."

"How?"

"His eyes were bloodshot."

"So?"

"If a person suffocates, blood rushes to the eyes and face and neck. There's a name for the effect, petechiae, according to my research. They are tiny pinpricks of red, sometimes even causing the eyes to be bloodshot. Your father's eyes were bloodshot."

"Huh? How do you know that?"

I hesitated, realizing I had given away too much, but the damage was done. If I told him Leo Cobb had found Odom dead, Ted would run to his cop cousin, Louis, and scream to high heaven. "You trust me, don't you, Ted?"

"Yeah. Sure. Why not?"

"Then just believe what I said. I've spoken with several individuals, and I've picked up a lot of information. Right now, I don't know what's true or false. I'm putting it all together. So, just trust me and don't ask any questions. All of this might lead nowhere. There's no sense in stirring anything up unnecessarily."

His eyes narrowed momentarily, and then he nodded. "Okay."

"Now, what time do you think Edna will be in?"

He shrugged. "She had some business to take care of. Probably one or two."

I changed the subject. "I had a nice little visit with your cousin, Lamia, last night down on the River Walk."

His eyes grew cold. "Oh?"

I studied him closely. "I had the feeling you two don't get along too well."

His eyes blazed. "You got that right."

"In fact, I heard that she was milking your uncle dry."

He pressed his lips together, and his eyes narrowed. "I don't know who told you that but they weren't too far off. Father finally had to put a stop to it but Lamia kept after him."

"You mean he cut off her financial support?"

He rolled his eyes. "Oh, no. Father would never do that. He was often mean and vindictive but he kept her allowance going. He just cut out the extras."

"What kind of allowance?"

"Five thousand a month."

I whistled softly.

He continued, his tone brusque. "She claims she can't get by on that. Well, she can. I do and she can too."

I struggled to hide my surprise at his sudden revelation. "That's quite a sum."

Through clenched teeth, he added, "She's always blown her money. Never been responsible."

Remembering how much he lost at the tracks, I wanted to say "And you are," but I suppressed the impulse. "You see her often?"

"No. Once a month maybe. It's just as well. We don't get along."

It didn't take a Dick Tracy to figure that out. "Does she have a career, a job, anything like that?"

"No, she lives on the money Father gives her." He chewed on his bottom lip a moment. "Maybe I shouldn't mention it because she is my cousin, but I think she might somehow be mixed up in the drug scene."

I played dumb. "Oh? How's that?"

A frown played over his colorless face. "Hard to say. There've been several late-night—when I say late, I mean two or three o'clock in the morning—calls for her. Once I ran into her on the River Walk. She was walking away from three or four of those long-haired street people—you know the kind that makes your stomach turn when you see them—dirty and greasy." He shivered. "They were glassy-eyed and slurred their words when they talked."

"What did she say?"

"She laughed it off. Said they were asking for a handout." He paused. "I know this might sound callous, but one positive thing came from Father's death."

"Oh?"

A derisive smile tightened his lips. "Yeah. As soon

as the will is probated, I don't figure we'll ever see her again."

"Splitsville, huh?"

His smile broadened. "Big time."

I gestured to the two prints on the wall between the bookcases. "What do you know about those prints?"

"Egyptian puzzles. Like I told you."

"Puzzles?"

"Yeah. From some tomb. He told me the name but it's slipped my mind. Some sort of hieratic writing from an obscure dynasty, Father said."

I didn't mention it but that was essentially the same thing Leo Cob had told me. I studied the puzzles, still struggling to remember what was so familiar about them. Suddenly, I saw what had been nagging at me. "If I remember right, he told Leo Cobb if he wanted the Piri Reis, he had to deal with these printings first."

Ted frowned. "I didn't know that."

"Well, your uncle did."

We studied the prints. "Any idea what he meant?"

Print Number One

Π෨෨෨෨෨෨ ✱ ✚   ψ☺Ջξ≏ℳ   ⵄ℩ℽ⯎Ͱℋℯℾ⅋   ෴෨

Print Number Two

෨෴Ϭℽ෴෴Ⅱ   ⴽ≏Ⅱ෴ℽ෨   ՋⅡ   Ϭ≏෨ℽ   ෴

Ted shook his head. "Not a one. There's nothing there. Like I said before, I took them apart. Nothing."

I glanced at him. "When I was talking to Edna, she said your father enjoyed puzzles."

Ted chuckled. "He loved them."

"Okay, now, let me get this straight. First, your father told you the map was located in the den. Right?"

"Yeah."

I held up another finger. "And second, according to Cobb, your father told him to get the Piri Reis he had to deal with these prints on the wall."

He lifted an eyebrow. "So?"

"So, Edna thinks the map might not even be in the den. She suggested that when your father told you it was located in the den, he was just trying to throw you off. That make sense?"

Ted shrugged. "I wouldn't be surprised. He liked to confuse people. All I know is that those prints are Egyptian puzzles—in some sort of obscure hieroglyphics is what he told me."

I studied them a moment longer, noticing a peculiar curiosity. I decided to play the devil's advocate. "How do you know that? Because he told you?"

"Yeah."

"Could he have lied to you about them? Maybe he told you that to simply stop you from asking questions."

With a sheepish grin, he replied, "I guess, but why would he do that?"

I chuckled. "Like I said, just to shut you up. To confuse you. Take a look at this." I pointed to a symbol in the first line, a four-pointed star. "I'm no expert. All I know about Egypt is that it has sand and mummies.

Now, I might be wrong, but I've never seen a star like that associated with ancient Egypt. Maybe it is. I don't know, but it's enough to make me wonder. And, a second thing is that I thought hieroglyphics was picture writing. This looks like an alphabet to me," I said, falling back on my years as an English teacher.

Ted frowned while I pulled out my note cards and looked around the den for the telephone. "Let's find out," I announced, picking up the receiver.

"What do you mean?"

Punching in the number of the Wingate Museum of Art from my note card, I explained, "I've never even heard of an Egyptian puzzle, have you?"

He arched an eyebrow. "Not until these."

The number rang. "So, let's see if George Moffit at the museum can put us in touch with an Egyptologist who can verify the fact that these printings could be puzzles."

Moffit gave me the name and number of the curator of Egyptian culture at the Claritin Museum of Cultural History in Dallas. I dialed the number. Five minutes later, I hung up and turned to Ted Odom. "He said somebody's pulling our leg, and the joker's name is Bernard Julius Odom."

Chapter Eighteen

T ed stared at me wide-eyed.

I explained. "To the best of the curator's knowledge, the puzzles enjoyed by the Egyptian royalty were word puzzles, not written ones like this."

Ted stared at me in disbelief. "Then what are these?" He took another step closer to the prints.

"It's obvious the map isn't hidden in the prints. From what Cobb said, I think the prints hold the secret to the location of the map. They are nothing more than puzzles your father made up." I had an idea, but I kept it to myself. I'd find out if my idea was right when I got back to my room.

His frown deepened. "You really think so?"

We moved closer to the two prints.

Print Number One

Ⴖ⧬⧬⧬⧬✻✦   ψ☺♌ξ⩵ⅲ   ⤢⅄⧬⧬Ⲏℯⲧ⅋   ☙

Print Number Two

⧬⧬℘Ⴘ⧬⧬Ⅱ   ℥⩵Ⅱ⧬Ⅵ⧬   ♌Ⅱ   ℘⩵⧬Ⅵ⧬

I pointed out the star in the first line.

Ted grunted. "I never paid any attention to it before."

"That's what your father counted on." I chuckled. "That's why he told everyone it was script from an obscure dynasty."

At that moment, my cell phone rang.

I didn't recognize the voice. "Boudreaux?"

"Yeah. Who's this?"

"That ain't important. You still looking for that map?"

I suppressed the sudden burst of excitement exploding through my veins. In a casual voice I said, "Yeah."

"If you are, come alone to room 223 at the Cattleman's Hotel next to the Alamo."

Before I could ask any questions, the caller hung up. Hastily I dialed star sixty-nine. A pay phone.

Ted frowned.

Stroking my chin thoughtfully, I considered the call. The only thing I hated worse than puzzles were blind calls. And this was one if I'd ever heard one. When you followed up on them, and you had to, you had no idea what you were walking into.

"So, what was that all about?"

I was suddenly aware of Ted staring at me. "Huh? Oh." I shook my head. "I don't know for certain. Some joker says he knows where the map is."

Ted's eyes grew wide. "Where?"

"He didn't say. He wants me to come to the Cattleman's Hotel."

He spun on his heel. "Let's go then."

"Alone."

Ted froze. "What?"

"That's what he said." I studied him a moment. "I don't think there's anything to this but I can't afford not to follow it up." I started for the door. "I'll stay in touch." I paused. "Oh. Do me a favor."

"Whatever."

"Make a copy of those prints and send them to my hotel. I want to work on them tonight."

The Cattleman's was one of the oldest hotels in San Antonio, appropriately named for the innumerable cattle barons and trail hands who frequented the establishment during the 1860s and 70s. And it had its requisite resident ghost, Ginny Mae, a chambermaid who, after a hundred and fifty-plus years, continued to look after rooms on the second and third floors.

Located across a narrow street from the Alamo, the white stucco building boasted wrought-iron balconies on all four floors except the first.

Jack pulled around the corner into the narrow street and parked in a loading zone. I hopped out. "Give me ten minutes. If I'm not back, come looking for me. Remember. Room 223."

He licked his lips nervously. "It sounds like some kind of setup to me, Tony."

"That's why I want you to come up in ten minutes. Of course," I added, "this bozo could be perfectly legitimate, but I don't want to take any chances."

Entering the Cattleman's lobby, I felt as if I had stepped back into an earlier century. The walls were festooned with western artifacts. Longhorns sporting needle-sharp horns spanning over eight feet peered down from the walls. Glancing around, I saw about half a dozen people in the lobby all wearing ten-gallon hats, a couple at the registration desk, a couple more ensconced in plush leather couches reading the newspaper, and two more heading into the Cattleman's Bar through a large arch. I climbed the wide stairs leading to the second floor, and found my way down the carpeted hallway to room 223.

I froze. Around the corner came a chambermaid carrying an armload of linens. Impossible, I told myself. Moments later she passed with a short nod and a bright smile. "Afternoon, sir." Sheepishly, I watched her disappear around the next corner.

Glancing up and down the empty hall, I knocked.

No answer.

I knocked again, and still no answer. My pulse picked up. Tentatively, I tried the doorknob. I wasn't surprised to find it turned easily.

Glancing up and down the empty hall once again, I hesitated. My good sense told me to get out of there as fast as I could, but the idiot part of me insisted I follow through on what I had come to do.

Like the imbecile, there is always one more idiot out there than you thought. This time, I was it. I pushed the door open and stepped inside and froze for the second time in as many minutes.

There, sprawled across the bed, lay Lamia Sue Odom. I'd seen enough corpses that I knew she was dead, but I shook her gently anyway, noting her arms were still warm. There were red marks on her throat. I checked her carotid. No pulse. I laid my ear to her chest. No heartbeat. I guessed she'd been dead less than an hour.

In that instant, I knew for certain Bernard Odom had been murdered just as I knew for certain someone had strangled Lamia Sue. I glanced around the room. There was no sign of struggle, which perplexed me. A victim just doesn't offer her assailant her throat and stand there. Maybe she'd been so toked up . . .

At that moment, an insistent honking from outside broke into my thoughts.

Then, through the open door, I heard thudding foot-steps, and in the background, sirens.

Without hesitation, I raced to the sliding doors, threw them open, stepped onto the balcony, then hastily closed them. Across the narrow street was the Alamo and its grounds, on which a large gathering of women were seated listening to a speaker. Down the street, I spotted

Jack in the Caddie. He waved and, with smoke pouring from his tires, sped toward me.

I swung over the balcony and, hanging by my fingers, dropped to the sidewalk. Luckily, those on the walk had heard the sirens and raced toward them.

Jack squealed to a halt and I jumped in. Moments later we were lost in the traffic.

"What's going on?" he shouted, whipping around the first corner, then pulling into the middle of the traffic. He worked his way to the outside lane, and then took the first street off the thoroughfare.

"You were right. It was a setup. You remember the young woman we talked to last night on the River Walk?"

Keeping his eyes on the traffic, he nodded. "What about her?"

"She's dead. Strangled."

He whistled. "And someone wanted you to take the fall, huh?"

"Looks that way."

"Where to now?"

"Back to the hotel." I had to find a refuge somewhere, where I could figure things out.

When Jack dropped me off, I paused before closing the car door. "If I were you, Jack, I'd get back to Austin. Someone might have got a description of your car."

With a sly grin, he retorted, "So? I was sightseeing downtown. I didn't do nothing illegal."

"All right, but listen. Anyone should ask, you called me to go sightseeing. We just drove around San Antonio for an hour or so, then spent another hour or two on the River Walk, nowhere in particular. Got it?"

"Yeah. I got it."

Climbing the stairs to my room, I grimaced at the fate of Lamia Sue. The Piri Reis would do her no good now. As soon as I could, I'd contact Ted and inform him of her death.

The light on my bedside phone was blinking. I called the operator. It was Dean Coggins from the university.

I called him back.

The dean was at a conference in Dallas. He bubbled with excitement. "I received word you wanted to speak with me about a donation to the department, Mr. Boudreaux. I'll be more than pleased to answer any questions you have. May I ask what you had in mind?"

"You're already familiar with it, Dean Coggins. The Piri Reis Map. As I understand it—"

"The what?"

"The Piri Reis Map. An ancient map from the sixteenth century." I paused, waiting for his response.

"I'm sorry, Mr. Boudreaux, but I've never heard of it."

"I beg your pardon?"

"I said I'd never heard of this map, whatever it is."

Sounding as contrite as I could, I apologized and explained. "My secretary must have made a mistake, Dean

Coggins. Perhaps it was the University of San Antonio who had asked for the Piri Reis. I'm sorry."

I hung up and leaned back, staring at the receiver. Papa Poggy had lied. He had told me the dean said the university could not pay such an exorbitant price. And that same dean had just told me he had never heard of the Piri Reis.

So why was the good father lying? And where was he those nights he left the classroom for a couple of hours?

Good questions all, and I planned to find out.

At that moment there came a knock at the door. I opened it, and a young bellhop handed me a sealed portfolio. "This just came for you, Mr. Boudreaux."

I tipped him a couple of bucks, then hurried back inside and opened the portfolio. The prints. Ted was on the ball.

Chapter Nineteen

Father Bertoldo Poggioreale's office was closed when I arrived at the campus. I stood outside the darkened office in frustration.

"The father's gone for the day," a cracked voice behind me said.

I looked around and an elderly woman in jeans and sweatshirt and holding a mop grinned at me, revealing two missing teeth in her uppers. "Just my luck," I said.

She cackled. "Ten minutes sooner, and you woulda caught him. He's been in his office all afternoon."

"You saw him, huh?"

She gestured to the spotless hallway. "Been stripping the floor. I been here since noon."

Well, at least, it appeared the good father had nothing to do with Lamia Odom's death. "You wouldn't happen to know where he lives, would you?"

She gestured out the door, the joints on her crippled hand knotted with arthritis. "Yes, sir. At the faculty dorm. Last one on the west end."

The sun had set by the time I found the dorm, and the wind had shifted to the north. A nip was in the air. Ten minutes later, Father Poggioreale stepped into the front lounge, a combination living room and recreation room. He grinned when he saw me. "Ah, Mr. Boudreaux. More questions?"

I went straight to the point. "First, the university knows nothing at all about the Piri Reis Map, which means obviously you wanted the map for yourself. And second, where did you disappear to those nights you left your evening class for a couple hours?"

His eyes wide in surprise, he inadvertently took a step backward. He parted his lips to speak but no words came. Finally, he managed to say, "I don't know what you're talking about. I—"

"Hold it, Father. Whatever is going on here is getting serious. There's a dead woman that someone is going to answer for, and it sure isn't going to be me."

His face blanched. "A—a dead woman? Who?"

"Someone who wanted the Piri Reis as much as you. I have proof you lied to me. Now, either come clean or I'm dumping all of this in the lap of the cops. You can play your silly little games with them."

He glanced around the cavernous room. No one else was present so he indicated a couch in the far corner.

After we sat, he whispered frantically. "I don't know

what's going on, but I had nothing to do with any-thing, and that's the truth."

"Then where were you those nights you left the classroom? October second to be specific."

His hands began to shake. "All right, I left the class-room but I didn't do anything."

"On October second, Bernard Odom died. I think he was murdered, and someone stole the Piri Reis. You wanted the map, and you have no alibi from seven thirty until nine forty-five."

Sweat popped out on his forehead, and he ran the tip of his tongue over his dry lips.

I added a little fuel to the fire. "A scandal would ruin you at this university. What parent will permit a child to go to a school with someone even suspected of murder and theft?"

He buried his face in his hands. "I didn't do any-thing. That's the truth."

"So, where were you?"

After a moment, he looked up, his face haggard with fear. "The truth is—if I tell you the truth, you won't tell the university, will you?'

"I don't make deals, Father, but if the truth has noth-ing to do with the maps or Odom, I can see nothing to be gained by mentioning it."

He nodded jerkily. "Okay, okay. Well, there's this young woman and—"

Immediately, I knew where he was going but I let him continue.

"And we've become very, ah, attached."

"Intimate?"

He hesitated then dropped his gaze to his lap. "Yes. We meet in the gym on Monday and Wednesday nights." His face was growing red. "And, well, you know."

"What's her name?"

Father Poggioreale grimaced. "I, ah, I can't say. It would ruin her."

"Not if it has nothing to do with the map." I hesitated, then gave him a figurative kick in the stomach. "But I'll ruin you if you don't tell me."

He grimaced in anguish. "Veronica Kinton. She teaches English here at the university."

I jotted her name down.

"What was it, Father? Just a physical thing between you two?"

His face blanched. "Oh, no. We're going to marry. With the profit from the map, we planned to move to the Cayman Islands where we would both teach. Interest income would make up the cut we would be taking in salaries."

I couldn't help admiring his ambition, but not the devious means for achieving it. "She lives in one of the dorms?"

He nodded. "The women's faculty dorm, next door."

"All right, and now the map. Why did you want it so bad as to make three offers?"

A chagrinned look spread over his face. "Three years ago in Spain, I met an industrialist who wanted the map. He would pay me a commission. He was willing to go as high as three million."

I frowned. "Hold on." I thumbed through my cards until I found the one for which I was searching. "According to Ted Odom, you offered two million for the map. Why not the full amount?"

His eyes held firm a moment. Then his gaze wavered and dropped to the floor.

"Oh." I understood. "You were planning on pocketing the difference plus the commission."

The good father nodded briefly.

"Who is this industrialist?"

He stared at me for several moments.

"You have to know?"

"If you don't want the cops in on this."

"Jorge Salazar in Madrid. He owns dozens of manufacturing firms."

I jotted the name on my notepad. "How can I contact him?"

The good father hesitated, then supplied me the information.

"That's all I need," I said, pushing to my feet.

He looked up hopefully. "You're not going to the police, are you? My reputation will be ruined if you do."

"Don't worry. If this holds up, there will be only three of us who know—me, you, and your conscience. No, make it four. Your lady friend. Now, let's go."

"Go? Where?"

"To the women's dorm."

He pushed to his feet, an obstinate gleam in his eyes. "Why?"

I shook my head. I felt no compassion or sympathy for the man. To me, the priesthood was a true calling from God, and to see someone desecrate that holy mission filled me with disgust. "Come on, Father. You think I'm going to take a chance on letting you call her and set up a story? No way. Now, are you coming, or do I call the police?"

Ten minutes later in the parlor of the dorm, Papa Poggy introduced me to Veronica Kinton, and then as I had previously instructed, left without another word.

Half a dozen ladies watched a TV in the corner. Another half dozen or so sat around the parlor. I suggested we go onto the porch.

She assured me Papa Poggy was telling the truth. "For the last few months, we've met like that."

"Haven't missed a night?"

"Sometimes, but not October second." She kept her eyes fixed on mine.

"How can you be absolutely certain?"

Her eyes wavered. Her bottom lip quivered, and she dropped her gaze to her feet. "Because the next morning was when I learned I was pregnant."

I lifted an eyebrow and nodded. "I see." Nodding to the male faculty dorm, I asked, "Why didn't he tell me that?"

Tears welled in her eyes. "He doesn't know yet."

"Oh." I whistled softly. The good father was in for a nice little surprise. He could kiss the Cayman Islands good-bye.

I glanced at my watch when I climbed in my Silverado. Six o'clock. Plenty of time to reach the Odom mansion before Edna left. By now, night had fallen over the city.

Chapter Twenty

When I turned the corner onto Fairchild Street, I spotted a woman climbing into a dark car on the far corner of the block. As I drew closer it sped away. I didn't get the license number. I didn't need to. The vehicle was a Rolls Royce.

Shivering against the chilly breeze, I knocked on the door. Ted opened it. I stepped inside and asked for Edna. "Just missed her. She just left in her cab."

The only vehicle I spotted was the Rolls. "Cab?"

"Yeah. Edna doesn't drive. She takes a cab to and from work."

I started to ask him if he knew of a taxi company that had a fleet of Rolls but decided to keep my mouth shut. Besides, I knew who owned a Rolls. What I couldn't figure was why Edna, if the woman I saw was her, was getting into a car with Joe Hogg? From what

I remembered of our earlier conversation, though brief, she had not much use for the man.

Ted shivered. "Care for a drink? It's getting cold out there. I think the temperature's dropped fifteen degrees in the last hour."

"Might as well." I didn't really care for a drink but I figured Ted was going to need one.

He led the way into the den. "Bourbon all right?"

"Yeah. Neat."

The books in one bookcase were stacked neatly on the floor. Over his shoulder, he explained. "I figured I might have overlooked something that would lead me to the map."

"What about the puzzles? Did you try to figure them out?"

He handed me my drink. He had the same, straight bourbon, no ice. With a sarcastic grunt he nodded to the books. "I don't know even where to begin. You have any luck?"

"Haven't started yet."

He plopped down on the couch and sipped his drink. "How did that telephone call work out? Any help?"

I studied him for a moment, searching for some body language that might suggest something other than the genuine concern he exhibited. "In a way."

Ted looked up at me expectantly.

"It wasn't good, Ted." I paused. "Get a grip." His brows knit in puzzlement. "Your cousin is dead."

He stared at me as if he hadn't understood my words. "What?"

I nodded. "She's dead. Lamia's dead. Someone strangled her."

He just continued staring at me without comprehension. "I—I don't understand. What?"

"The phone call, Ted. The one about the map. It was a setup."

"But—Lamia? Why, she—"

"I'm surprised the cops haven't contacted you yet. That means whoever killed her removed all identification, so it'll take some time to ID her."

He buried his face in his hand. "I can't believe it."

"It's true. And I'm telling you something else you can believe. Your father was murdered also. Something is going on around here that neither of us knows about." I hesitated and stared at the thinning hair on his bowed head suspiciously. "At least, I don't know about it."

The sharp tone in my voice caused him to look up. "What are you saying? You think I had something to do with all this?"

I studied him for several moments. "I'm going to tell you something, Teddy boy. Anyone who can lay down five or ten grand on the nags has reason to worry if his father has been murdered, especially since his father was rich."

His face blanched. "What are you talking about? I'll have you know that—"

"Cut it out, Teddy. I talked to Patsy Fusco. You've been playing the horses for ten years." I paused. "When it comes to stealing the map, you don't fit. It's yours. But when it comes to the murder of your father, your half-million inheritance plus your gambling history makes you one juicy suspect. You follow me, Teddy boy?"

I didn't think his face could grow any whiter, but it did. He jerked his head from side to side in denial. He gulped down the remainder of his bourbon, then scurried across the floor to pour another. "I tell you, I had nothing to do with it," he said over his shoulder.

"That remains to be seen."

He turned to face me. He fought to contain the panic evident in his eyes. "All right. I gamble. I've lost thousands, hundreds of thousands, but I did not kill my father."

I sipped my bourbon. Smooth, but then rich people always buy quality booze—if not for the taste then for the prestige of brand. "The police will come see you, Teddy. If not tonight, tomorrow. If you ever want to find the Piri Reis, you forget I told you about Lamia's murder."

He frowned.

I explained. "Listen to me carefully. I was the fall guy today. When I entered room 223, I found Lamia on the bed. She had been strangled. Moments later the police arrived. That was too convenient. I managed to duck out ahead of them."

The perplexed look on his face told me he wasn't following me.

As simply as I once labored to explain the difference in nouns and pronouns to my tenth grade English students back in Madison High, I explained the situation to Teddy. "If I had been caught in there, it would have taken weeks, months to straighten it all out. Those would be months lost in finding the Piri Reis, which in turn would give whoever is after it that much more time. Now do you understand?"

He nodded slowly. "Yeah. Now I see."

"When the investigators get here, don't make up anything. Tell them the truth. Just don't let them know you were aware of her murder. You understand?"

He nodded slowly. "Yeah."

I studied him another moment, my misgivings mounting. I wished I had said nothing to him about Lamia's murder but the damage was done.

Just as I headed for the door, the bell rang. Ted and I exchanged frantic looks. He nodded and gestured to the kitchen. "Out the back."

I wasted no time. Five minutes later, I was on the sidewalk outside the mansion. Staying in the shadows, I circled the block. I froze at the corner, spotting two darkened vehicles in front of the house.

Crossing the street, I made my way to my pickup and moments later vanished into the traffic. I whistled softly. Cutting it close, Tony, I told myself as I slowed for a signal light at the end of the block.

Traffic, surprisingly enough, was light. I wondered about Lamia. Who would have something to gain by killing her and blaming it on me? I knew the *why* but the *who* slipped through my fingers just like I was trying to grab water.

Cobb didn't think much of her, I reminded myself,

remembering his remarks concerning the dead woman. Maybe I needed to pay him another visit. See what else he knew or had to say about Lamia Odom. I glanced at the clock on the radio. Almost 8:30. For a moment, I vacillated between visiting Cobb tonight or waiting until in the morning.

Pulling into the parking lot of the inn, I decided to wait, reminding myself that Janice was to arrive around noon the next day. If I left early next morning for Cobb's place, I would be back in time to meet her. I hesitated, realizing I had given no further thought to her suggestion of marriage. In a way, I dreaded the next day.

Back in my room, I pulled out the portfolio Ted had sent and retrieved the copies of the prints. Now, I hate puzzles, but that doesn't mean I can't work them. A few years earlier, I'd had to figure out a couple to help me find a missing teenager whose body had been hidden in a barrel of aging bourbon for years.

Booting up, I went online and into my folder of favorites where I pulled up my code-breaking manual. I glanced at the puzzles once again.

Print Number One

Π🙢🙠🙟🙣✽✦ ψ♋♌ξ♎♏ ♐♑♒♓🙰🙵 🙱🙲

Print Number Two

🙢♒🙨♉♒♒♊ 🙩♎♊♒♑🙣 ♌♊ 🙨♎🙢♑♒

Back at the mansion, I'd taken a wild guess that the symbols were nothing more than transitional ciphers—that is, pictorial characters substituted for alphabetical characters. And now, the more I studied them, the more firmly convinced I became that I was right. The old man had just claimed they were hieroglyphics from an obscure era to throw off everyone.

Now, all I had to do was figure out which symbols stood for which characters; but that proved to be as simple as stacking BBs.

For the next half hour, I cataloged the frequency of the symbols in the first print, then tried to match them with the frequency of the letters in the alphabet.

To my growing frustration, I ended up with only gibberish, which is the most forgiving and generous adjective to describe the resulting answer, RDDOB AECDUF TPHXNS BAZ.

I leaned back and studied the symbols in the puzzle again. I'd seen some of them before, but where?

Suddenly, an idea hit me.

I pulled up my word processing program and went to the Insert Symbol chart. Those symbols were similar. In fact two or three matched those of Bernard Odom but that was it. They signified nothing.

The feeling gnawed at me that I was staring straight at the answer but was too blind to see it. On impulse, I went to the help function on my word processor and pulled up symbols, thinking perhaps something there might jostle my memory.

I couldn't help noticing several of the help options

referred to Fonts, so I immediately accessed the font menu and scrolled down through it.

When I hit the W fonts, I caught my breath. There were four: Webdings, Wingdings, Wingdings 2, and Wingdings 3.

I held my breath. Was this the solution, something this simple? Quickly, I typed the alphabet in each font. Upon comparing them to the puzzles, I realized Odom had used a combination of symbols from each font.

Print Number One

Π☙☙☙☙☙✱✦ ψ☺♌ξ♎♏ ✗♑♒♓♯☌♒ ☪

For an hour, I struggled to make some sense of the puzzle. I transposed letters, substituted numerals and various ciphers for letters. Nothing worked.

I leaned back in my chair and studied the characters. What if the first puzzle was intended to be nothing but gibberish? What if Odom deliberately set it up, guessing that whoever tried to translate it would figure the second puzzle was gibberish just like the first?

I turned to the second puzzle.

Print Number Two

☙♒♌♊♒♒Π ♌♎Π♒♑♒☙ ♌Π ♌♎☙♑♒

To my surprise, I had a little better luck. Using a combination of Wingding, Webding fonts and symbols, I came up with a partial translation that meant nothing:

EH__HH_ _D_H__ __ _DE_H_

Shaking my head, I muttered a soft curse.

There was only one answer. Puzzle King Bernard Julius Odom had tossed another puzzle into the mix.

I shook my head, frustrated. I tossed my pencil aside. I'd give it another shot later. Right now I needed sleep.

Chapter Twenty-one

The restaurant patio of the Grand Isle Inn overlooked the River Walk. I was enjoying coffee and a short stack of pancakes in the brisk air next morning when a shadow fell over the table. I glanced up into the unsmiling face of an aging man in cowboy boots, washed-out jeans, and a pearl-button western shirt over which he wore a red windbreaker with the name Houston Texans on it.

"Tony Boudreaux?" His voice was gravelly.

I nodded. "Yeah?"

He flashed a badge. "Charley Newton. San Antonio PD." He slid into the empty chair across the table. "Mind if I sit?"

I chuckled. "Would it do me any good if I did?"

He shrugged his rounded shoulders. "Probably not."

"Then by all means, Charley. Sit." I waved for the waiter and pointed to the coffee. "How'll you have your coffee?"

"Black." He leaned back. "You know someone by the name of Lamia Sue Odom?"

"Yeah."

"What's your business with her?"

I sipped my coffee and grinned. "Didn't Teddy Odom tell you?"

A flicker of his lips that might have passed for a grin vanished. "Yeah, but I want to hear what you got to say."

"Probably nothing to add. Teddy hired me to find a map, the Piri Reis. There were several interested it the map, Lamia Sue Odom among them. I talked to her a couple days ago down on the River Walk below her hotel, the Elena Towers. I haven't spoken with her since. Can I ask why all the questions?"

"Where were you yesterday afternoon?"

"Have I done something?"

He looked up as the waiter set the coffee in front of him. "Not that I know of. So where were you?"

"Well, for your information, I left the Odom mansion around two or two thirty. A friend and I drove around sightseeing for an hour or so."

"Such as?"

I shrugged. "Just driving around. The city is full of sights. We just—"

"What's this friend's name and where can I find him?"

I gave him Jack's name and the hotel. "If he's checked out, you can find him in Austin. There's only one Jack Edney in the phone book."

With a grunt, he nodded. "All right. After you left this friend of yours, then what?"

"Then I paid a visit to Father Bertoldo Poggioreale out at the University of Grace and Brotherhood."

"What about?"

"The map. I didn't leave him until after dark. Now, can you tell me what's going on?"

He grunted. "Lamia Sue Odom was found dead yesterday."

I grimaced. "Hate to hear that. I didn't know her except for our one visit. Does her cousin know yet?"

"Yeah. That's how we got onto you."

I played dumb. "Oh, yeah. I didn't think about that."

Charley narrowed his eyes. "I bet." He cleared his throat. "All right, Mr. Boudreaux. That's all I need right now." He looked down at me. "You'll be around?"

"If I'm not, Charley, you can get me in Austin. I'm in the phone book just like Jack."

He glanced at his untouched coffee. "And thanks for the coffee."

I grinned. "Any time."

After Newton left, I decided to pay Leo Cobb a visit. Other than Ted Odom, he was the only one who had expressed a dislike for Lamia Odom.

Thirty minutes later, I rang the doorbell at the Cobb house. The first echoes hadn't died away when it jerked open and Martha Cobb stared up at me, the expectation on her distraught face fading into disappointment. "Oh, Mr. Boudreaux. I thought it was Leo." She wrung her hands.

"He isn't here?"

"No. I haven't seen him since noon yesterday, and I'm worried sick."

I just stared at her, unable to believe what I had walked into. One dead and one missing. What was going on with that blasted map? "When did you see him last?"

"Yesterday, around noon. I was out tending the flowerbed in back when he came out and told me he had some business—" She hesitated and glanced around. Realizing we were standing on the porch where the whole neighborhood could hear us, she invited me. "I'm sorry, Mr. Boudreaux. I just wasn't thinking. Please, come in. Can I get you some coffee or lemonade?" she asked over her shoulder as she led the way into the den.

"No, thanks."

She sat on the couch and looked up at me, her eyes pleading for help. "Leo said he had business to take care of. Important business that couldn't wait."

I kept thinking about Lamia Sue sprawled on the bed in the Cattleman's. Was that the business? If so, why? "Did he tell you what it was?"

"No."

"Didn't you think that was strange?"

She frowned at me, then forced a weak smile. "Oh, no. Leo takes care of all our business. He doesn't want to worry me about things. That's why I was surprised when you mentioned the mortgage company foreclosing on our house." She paused. Her face grew more intense. "After you left, Leo promised me he'd take care of the mortgage trouble."

I nodded, thinking Cobb should have his rear kicked for not realizing just what a trusting wife he had. "Has he ever done anything like this before? I mean, spending the night away without telling you?"

"Oh yes. Several times."

If that were so, why was she so upset this time? I asked her.

"Because of the news."

"News?"

"Yes. Channel Eleven this morning. Lamia Sue Odom was found dead in a hotel room." Her eyebrows turned down, and she chewed on her bottom lip.

Mrs. Leo Cobb really had me confused. "So, why should her death worry you so much?"

Anguish filled her eyes. She hesitated, chewing on her bottom lip. Finally, she blurted out, "Because Lamia Sue Odom was blackmailing Leo!"

Talk about the proverbial kick in the teeth. I think I staggered back one or two steps. I stammered for words, then managed the eloquent response, "What?"

She nodded woodenly. "For the last two years or so."

With her revelation, several of the questions I had about Cobb's financial situation suddenly made sense. While his income had dropped after losing the slander case, the loss of income did not appear so severe as to warrant losing his house. "How much?"

"Two thousand a month. Cash."

"She picked it up?"

With a sheepish grin, she mumbled, "We usually met wherever she said."

I nodded slowly. Take off twenty-four thousand a year from his income, and I could see why he had trouble with his mortgage payment. That also answered another question festering in my simple mind. I had wondered how she maintained her lifestyle on the five thousand a month Odom gave her. Her plush suite in the Elena Towers was at least twenty-five hundred. Patsy Fusco had said she was only a small-time stringer.

Now, I knew.

And that answer gave birth to another question. If she was blackmailing Cobb, could she have been doing the same to others? "Two thousand a month, huh?"

"Yes."

"Why? I mean, what did she have on him?"

"You already know about it."

I arched an eyebrow. "Oh, that Seventeenth Dynasty vase twenty years ago up in Seattle."

She nodded.

"How did she find out?"

Martha Cobb shook her head slowly, her straw-like gray hair bobbing behind her. "We've never figured that out."

"So, you've no idea where he is?"

She wrung her hands. Tears glittered in her eyes. Her frail voice quivered. "I'm afraid what he might have done."

My sentiments exactly. I drew a deep breath. I had to go to the police with this.

At that moment, the front door opened, and a bellowing voice called out, "Martha? It's me. I'm home."

She and I looked at each other in stunned amazement.

A sneer played over Cobb's face when he entered the den. "So, Boudreaux. To what do we owe the pleasure of your visit this time?"

Martha jumped to her feet. "Leo! Where have you been? I've been worried sick."

He looked at her in surprise. "I told you I had some business. What's the problem?"

His cavalier attitude bristled the hair on the back of my neck. "I'll tell you what the problem is, Leo old boy. The little lady who has been blackmailing you has been murdered, so you better have yourself one good alibi, or you're going to have one heck of a job to keep from riding the needle up in Huntsville."

Cobb gaped at me in disbelief as he struggled to absorb my words. He turned to his wife. "What's going on?"

"I was scared for you, Leo. When I heard she was dead, I remembered you telling me that you were going to take care of business. I was afraid that you might have . . ."

He closed his eyes and slumped into an upholstered chair. "You ought to know better than that, Martha. I couldn't do anything like that. I swear on our daughter's head. I had nothing to do with it." He looked up at me. "It's the truth. A guy called about the Piri Reis. Wanted me to meet him at the roadside park at the top of the Devil's Backbone northwest of San Marcos. I waited and waited but he never showed up."

"That's convenient."

He heard the sarcasm in my tone. "You think I'm lying?"

I studied him a moment. "It isn't what I think, Leo. You've got nothing to back up your claim. No one was with you. No one saw you. If I had to make a choice one way or another, I'd say 'yes, you're lying.'"

"But it's the truth. There's a table at the park and a trash can off to one side."

I chuckled. "There's probably ten thousand roadside parks in Texas with a table and trash can off to one side."

Frustration clouded his eyes. "Look, there was a store nearby. A white wooden building. One side is like a general store. The other is a liquor store. The old geezer running it looks like he's a hundred. A full head of white hair. I went in there around five thirty. I bought two Dr Peppers and a bag of Oreo cookies. I threw them in the trashcan when I finished. You can talk to him."

Eyes blazing, Martha asked, "Why didn't you call? At least I wouldn't have worried so much."

"I tried, but Devil's Backbone is in the middle of nowhere. Nothing around but live oak and cedar trees. I couldn't get any cell phone service, and what few stores are around close down at six o'clock. Besides, I've told you. Nothing's going to happen to me. No sense in you worrying."

"She does have to worry, Leo," I reminded him. "And if you've got any sense, you'd better do some worrying too. Right now, you're a dandy suspect."

He furrowed his brow, his eyes studying mine intently. He pushed to his feet. "I told you the truth, and I can prove it." He went to the answering machine beside his phone. "I wasn't here when he called yesterday, so he left a message." He punched the rewind button. Moments later, a guttural voice said, "Cobb, if you're interested in the Piri Reis, call me at 512-555-6720 at exactly eleven o'clock." The machine clicked off. "I checked the phone number. It's a pay phone on the north side of town. So, I called him. He wanted to meet at the Devil's Backbone at four o'clock. But he never showed up. I started to leave half a dozen times but I kept hoping he might show up. He never did."

His wife looked up at me with hope glowing in her eyes. "That proves he wasn't here, doesn't it, Mr. Boudreaux?"

"All it proves is that there's a message on the answering machine. You want me to tell you what the cops will say? They'll say you paid some joker five bucks to call and leave the message."

Martha Cobb's face crumpled into tears. Cobb put his arm around her shoulders to console her.

"Look, if it'll make you two feel any better, I believe you."

He looked at me gratefully.

"But, I'm going to have to verify your story. This old man, is he the only one who saw you?"

Cobb considered for a moment. "Well, there were others who passed and waved, but—I suppose he's the only one I know how to get in touch with."

I smiled at Mrs. Cobb. "I'll check on his alibi. If it holds up, then you've caught a lucky break. I should be back before dark."

Chapter Twenty-two

On the way to the hotel, I ran back over the events of the last few days. As soon as I figured out the last twist Odom put in his puzzle, I'd have the Piri Reis.

I was convinced that Odom and his niece were both murdered, and the killer or killers were after the map. With that little assumption in place, then the efforts to scare me off—the eighteen-wheeler, the tossed room, the planted coke, the gunman, and the setup—all made sense.

What had begun as a simple search for a map had turned into a double murder. I knew I should pay a visit to Chief Louis Ibbara and reveal what I knew. But then, I reminded myself that I really knew nothing, not for certain. All I had, with one exception, were neat little theories with no proof. The one exception was Leo

Cobb, and later that afternoon, I would find out if he could have strangled Lamia Sue or not.

I set her death at sometime between three and three thirty. Probably closer to the former for when I arrived at four, her body was already cooling.

Janice was waiting for me when I reached my room. She was casually dressed in brown slacks and a beige blouse that set off her dark eyes. Her brown hair was parted in the middle and framed her face like a heart.

She stood on tiptoe and curled her arms around my neck. "I've missed you," she purred, touching her lips to mine.

I'd be lying if I said the marriage business was not in the back of my mind, but then, the tingle of electricity when her lips touched mine reminded me just how much I had missed her. "That goes double for me."

I could feel her lips curl into a smile. She pulled back slightly and arched an eyebrow. "You have the most romantic way of putting things, Tony."

I saw the teasing glitter in her eyes. "Hey," I retorted with a laugh, "that's one of the lines Casanova always used." I swatted her playfully on the derriere. "You ought to be grateful I'm such a sophisticated lover."

She laughed and gracefully stepped back. "So, what do you have in mind for us this afternoon?"

I relaxed slightly. "How about a drive through the hill country in your Jag? Weather's perfect. Couple of hours, then drinks, a light dinner on the River Walk, and then join the annual Mexican Bracero Festival here at the hotel."

Janice is rich, obscenely rich, but in all fairness she wears her cloak of wealth without a great deal of posturing. She laughed brightly and touched a manicured fingernail to my forehead. "You must have read my mind. I brought the Miata instead of the Jag. It's a lot more fun to drive on days like this."

I laughed and hugged her to me. "Then let's get with it."

We headed north on I-35 in her three-year-old Miata. I had questioned her when she bought the XK Jag as to why she hadn't swapped the Miata in. Her retort was a typical rich child's response: "It's cute, and it's more fun than the Jaguar."

Years back, I had ridden in a friend's reconditioned MG, a 1953 model. The unique little car shuddered and bounced over bumps, and when you hit ripples in the highway, it was like sliding down an old fashioned washboard.

The Miata, in that respect, was the MG reincarnated.

But none of that mattered when we hit the winding two-lane Farm to Market asphalt road carrying us deep into the hill country out of San Marcos. There were several sharp S-curves that the little Miata manipulated effortlessly.

Most of the vehicles we met were pickups, many four-wheel drives, several off-roaders.

Ancient live oaks starting to lose their leaves lined the road. Occasional maples and sweet gum and pecan displayed patches of red and gold among the panorama of green.

"It's beautiful out here," Janice called out over the roar of the wind.

I glanced at her. She was leaning back against the headrest, the wind whipping the ends of her hair in her eyes. "Yeah."

She turned her head on the seat and look at me, an amused look in her eyes. "Any particular reason for coming this way?"

Janice could read me like a book. That's probably because I'm as complicated as a primary reader. You know the one. "See Jane. See Jane run."

With a grin, I said, "Well, now that you mention it."

She laughed. "I thought so. What's going on?"

I flexed my fingers about the wheel of the little car. "Nothing much. I just need to find out if one old boy was out here yesterday afternoon."

A sign on the shoulder of the road read DEVIL'S BACKBONE 3. "That's where we're heading." I glanced at my watch. Almost an hour since we left the hotel.

"Devil's Backbone." She feigned a shiver. "Brrr. Sounds ominous."

The winding road began to climb. A couple of minutes later, we found ourselves speeding along the crest of one of the six hump-backed ridges rising several hundred feet above the hardwood forests below. Stunted live oak and scrawny cedar dotted the steep slopes of the individual ridges. On either side of the road were guardrails between the shoulder and the steep drop-offs.

Looking at the ridges, I couldn't fathom the inspiration for the word "backbone," unless whoever named it pictured the devil bending so far over backward that the back of his head touched his heels.

At the top of the first ridge was a roadside park, the one Cobb had mentioned. I pulled off and climbed out.

Janice followed, standing on the concrete slab on which the picnic table stood. A spreading live oak shaded the table, and a crisp breeze slithered across the crest of the ridge. She peered out over the valley below that spread to the horizon. "It's beautiful up here."

"Yeah," I replied, my head stuck in the fifty-five gallon barrel serving as a trash container. I saw no sign of the Oreo package or the empty Dr Pepper cans.

I glanced around and spotted a broken branch about three feet long. Using it, I stirred the first level of trash and spotted a wadded up Oreo bag and two crushed Dr Pepper cans. Maybe Cobb was telling the truth. I fished out an empty plastic bag, and then using the branch, managed to dump the crushed bag and cans in it. If they were Cobb's, his prints would be on them. Now all I had to do was establish a definite time.

"How about something to drink? There's a store down the road apiece."

"Never mind," she replied, turning to me with a twinkle in her eyes. "I came prepared." She pulled the passenger seat forward and extracted an insulated bag from which she produced a bottle of Zinfandel and two Styrofoam cups. She held one up. "I know it's an unforgivable social sin to drink wine from a foam cup, but at least the law won't know what it is." She smiled wickedly.

I laughed and hugged her, then quickly poured us a drink. "I've got to stop down there at the store anyway. Won't take but a minute."

A rock-jawed redneck with a week-old beard and knotted fists glared at me from behind the counter. "Old Jake is the one you need to see. He run this here place yesterday. He took off this afternoon."

"He live around here?"

He stared at me. For a moment, I didn't think he was going to reply, but then he nodded. "Go on up the highway here about two miles. Farm Road 3314 heads back to the lake. Take a left there. His place is the first road to the right."

I thanked him and started to leave, but he stopped me. "If you're going to see old Jake, he won't talk to you."

Turning back with a frown, I asked why.

With an amused twist on his lips, he said, "Jake's kinda odd. He don't like outsiders. You want to talk to him, you got to take a bottle of whiskey for him and his pets." He nodded to the package store next door.

I studied the grinning man for several seconds. If ever I'd seen a rip off, this was one, but I didn't want to take the chance. "Whatever you say." I reached for the glass door opening into the package store.

"You can't go through that one," he exclaimed. "You got to go outside and come through the front door."

Standing there, holding the door partially open, I stared at him. "Do what?"

He shrugged. "It's the law. Package store's got to have a single entrance for customers. He nodded to the front door. Go out and come in the door over there. I'll meet you there." He stepped through the door I was holding open and pulled it shut behind him.

All I could do was shake my head and do as he said.

While a couple of years had passed since I bought a fifth of Jim Beam Black Label, I knew inflation had not kicked it up to twenty bucks a bottle, which is what I had to pay. I held up the bottle. "You guarantee this will do the trick?"

He leered at me. "It's the only thing, friend."

Old Jake's place was a quarter of a mile back in the woods, a doublewide mobile home sitting on concrete blocks in the middle of two acres of rusted hulks of cars and pickups, broken down riding mowers, and half a dozen skeletons of various brand tractors being scavenged for parts. A face appeared at a window when we pulled up. Moments later, a wizened old man shuffled onto the porch and squinted at us.

I waved and stepped out, under my breath telling Janice to stay put. "Jake?"

Saying nothing, he eyed me suspiciously.

"The old boy at the store told me where I could find you."

Taking a few steps closer, I held up the bottle of Jim Beam. "I brought a present for you."

The mistrustful expression on his face broke into a grin. He waved to me. "Then come on in, sonny. And bring your girl."

"That's all right. She'd—"

"No, no. Bring her in." He called out to Janice. "Come on in, young lady. We'll break open the bottle."

I looked around at her helplessly.

She lifted her eyebrows and shrugged as if to say "Why not?" She climbed out.

The mobile home smelled musty. It wasn't quite like the moldy smell of straw in a barn. The smell was familiar, but I couldn't place it. We sat at the kitchen table while Jake poured us stiff drinks in dingy tumblers. Janice eyed hers warily, and I wouldn't have been surprised to see a crew of bugs sailing a boat in my bourbon.

He downed his in one gulp then poured himself another. "Now, what can I do for you two?"

"Yesterday afternoon. Did an outsider come in to the store and buy Dr Peppers and Oreos?"

He pursed his thin lips. "That all you want to know?"

I grinned. "That's all."

"Sure did. Kinda fat. Not much hair. Sweats a lot. He come in just before closing and bought two Dr Peppers and a bag of Oreo cookies. I don't know what he was up to but he'd been sitting up at the roadside park almost all day."

With a sigh of relief, I relaxed. Leo Cobb had just been cleared. Good news for him, bad for me, although his innocence narrowed the field of suspects. "I don't know if anyone else is going to want to ask you about this guy or not. They might."

He chuckled. "I got no objection long as they bring a bottle for me and my pets."

I glanced at Janice who had taken a couple of dainty sips from her tumbler just to be polite. "Yeah, the old boy at the store said you had pets." I glanced around. "I don't see them. What are they? Dogs, cats? You got them outside?"

His eyes twinkled. "Yep, I got my share of no-good hounds, but they ain't pets. No, sir, my pets, I keep 'em in the house." He tapped sharply on the table several times and peered at the couch in the living room. "Jefferson Davis oughta be coming out anytime now."

Suddenly, from under the couch popped the head of a black snake as big around as my wrist, which proceeded in leisurely slithers across the floor toward us. Behind me, I heard Janice gag. "Tony!"

"Don't worry none," Jake said. "He's an old rat snake, and he ain't going to hurt no one. He just wants a drink." Taking a shallow saucer from the table, he put it on the floor and splashed a dollop of bourbon in it. "Just don't make no sudden moves and scare the little feller."

Little feller? Jefferson Davis was six feet long if he were an inch. Besides, I couldn't have made a sudden move if I'd wanted to but I did manage to down the rest of my bourbon in one gulp. I glanced around at Janice who was also knocking down her drink, dingy tumbler or not. If I could have stilled my shaking hand, I would have poured myself another drink.

Without bothering to look at us, the black snake paused at the saucer, then began slurping at the whiskey.

Jake reached down and stroked the snake. "I got more in the bedroom. You folks want to see them?"

Eyes fixed on the rat snake, Janice and I rose and slowly backed away. "No, thanks, Jake. I appreciate your help. And don't get up. We can show ourselves out."

Chapter Twenty-three

Back in the car, we gulped down our cups of wine and refilled them once again.

Janice groaned and shivered. "Snakes! Ughh! Can you imagine living with snakes?"

We headed back to Devil's Backbone, ready to get back to San Antonio. I glanced at my watch. Almost three. Yep, I told myself, I could eliminate Cobb from the murder of Lamia Sue. First, he was up here all afternoon, and second, he couldn't possess the map, for that was the reason he had driven to Devil's Backbone.

Just as we reached the narrow stretch of road on the crest of Devil's Backbone, a bright red off-roader sitting about three feet off the ground roared out of a side road heading directly for us.

Janice screamed. "Tony!"

One of the advantages of the Miata is instant, and I mean instant, acceleration. I tromped the pedal, and the small car shot forward. Behind us, tires squealed. I glanced in the rearview to see the large Ford pickup bounce off a guardrail, then back up and take after us. By now, we were almost half a mile ahead.

Janice looked at me in alarm. "Tony! What's going on? What was that all about?"

I shook my head, keeping my attention focused on the road ahead. The little twin-cam, four-cylinder engine put out a hundred and forty horsepower, and I was whipping every one of those horses as hard as I could, but slowly the big off-roader drew closer.

We were lucky. Most of the traffic on the narrow road was coming our way. After-work traffic, I guessed. Ahead, I spotted an S-curve. I glanced in the rearview and my heart jumped into my throat. The sneering grill of the off-roader was snarling down at us. Then we hit the curve.

The Miata swept through it like it was tied to the road. When we hit the straightaway, the Ford pickup was a hundred yards back. Even as I watched, the pickup leaped forward. I noticed there was no front license plate. Through the windshield of the off-roader, I spotted a rectangular shape on the rear window. A dealer's plate.

That's when I remembered the eighteen-wheeler the previous Tuesday that ran me off the road. It also had a dealer's license on its rear window.

Janice was gripping the dash so hard, her knuckles were white. My brain raced. Once we left the S-curves, we were dead meat.

We sped through a couple more S-curves, picking up distance, then quickly losing it. As we came out of the last curve, I spotted a pickup at a three-way intersection waiting for us to pass.

And then I had a crazy idea as we flashed past a road sign indicating another three-way intersection a mile ahead. The Miata couldn't outrun the big Ford, but it could outmaneuver it.

"Hold on," I muttered through clenched teeth.

Janice looked at me in alarm.

"We're turning left up ahead." I began slowly to back off the accelerator.

She cut her eyes at the rapidly approaching pickup. "Hurry, Tony. He's catching us. Don't slow down!"

Slowing still more, I muttered, "That's what I want."

Her eyes grew wide. "You what?"

Teeth clenched, I flexed my fingers about the wheel. "You'll see. Just hold on."

By now, the Ford pickup was less than thirty yards back. I could have sworn the chrome grill was leering in anticipation. The turnoff loomed ahead. I slowed more. In the rearview, I saw the driver's snarling grin.

I figured all he wanted to do was nudge us with those overgrown tires, but he was the one in for a surprise.

Fortunately, the intersection was empty. We were less than a hundred yards from it. Moments later, we reached it. At the last moment, I tapped the brakes and turned the wheel. As if fastened to the end of a chain, the little roadster whipped around the corner, tires squealing slightly, the rear end threatening to break loose. Quickly, I corrected for the slide.

Behind us, we heard an ear-splitting screech of rubber. I was too busy getting the Miata back in the right lane to pay attention to what was taking place behind.

Janice gasped. "Tony!"

Then I heard a load thump, and the chilling shriek of metal against asphalt and gravel ripped through the wind buffeting my ears. I glanced into the rearview mirror to see the off-roader sliding to a halt on its side off the shoulder of the road. I blew out through my lips. "That was close," I muttered.

Sagging back in her seat, Janice groaned. "Don't tell me. That had something to do with the case you're working on?"

With a sheepish grin, I nodded. "Having second thoughts about coming down here?"

She studied me for a moment, a wry expression drawing tiny lines in her forehead. She glanced at the floorboard for the cup she had dropped when the off-roader jumped us. Without a word, she filled it with Zinfandel, and offered it to me. "Not a bit," she replied with a broad smile.

Throughout the remainder of the drive into San Antonio, the dealer's license on both the off-roader and the eighteen-wheeler nagged at me. Obviously, the same individual was behind both attempts to scare me off.

Now, I'm not too swift, but one name leaped into

my head. There was only one person among the suspects who I knew might have the contacts for the off-roader and the eighteen-wheeler—Joe Hogg.

But why? Just so he could have some university name a building after him? He might be crass and crude and coarse, but he was sharp enough not to take a chance on riding the needle by murdering two people.

Still, I planned on another talk with Mr. Hogg.

After dinner, we headed back to the Grand Isle Inn where the tenth annual Bracero Festival was in full swing. And we were swept up in the gala festivities until just after ten when Janice's cell phone rang.

Her aunt had been taken back to the hospital.

Ten minutes later, I stood in front of the inn, staring at the taillights of her Miata disappearing into the traffic. Part of me was relieved she had mentioned nothing about marriage, but curiously enough, another part of me was disappointed. Had I done something to make her change her mind?

Puzzled at my own feelings, I turned back to the hotel. And I had always thought women were hard to figure.

Instead of basking in the wonderful afterglow of an unforgettable night with Janice, I spent the morning with a pot of coffee and two bagels trying to nail down exactly where I stood on the case, since, in my thick-headed opinion, it had escalated from theft to murder.

Leo Cobb, who had been one of my main suspects, I put on the back burner. Of course there was always the possibility he had an accomplice, and the Devil's Backbone was nothing more than an elaborate alibi. But I didn't think so. I could be wrong but Cobb didn't strike me as being that inventive.

Of course, he was at Odom's the night of the old man's death. That he admitted. He didn't have to, for no one had seen him. If he had killed Odom, the last thing he would admit was being there.

Ervin Maddox had the opportunity. His whereabouts were unaccounted for around the time of the murder. Motive? Jealously initiates many regrettable and foolish acts. I figured he was a good prospect, depending on just where he was after disappearing from the museum. I checked my notes. From around a little after eight to nine o'clock, he was missing. I paused, peering into space and wondering if the cab driver, Casey, had turned up. I jotted a note to call him that afternoon to identify Ervin Maddox as his fare that night at 2112 Fairchild.

Then there was Hogg. With him it was ego, a drive, a desire to possess that which very few could. The map was simply a means to an end, his name immemorial on some brick-and-glass edifice on a university campus. And he was, by his own admission, outside the mansion. I doubted if he went inside, for Edna would have noticed him.

And speaking of Edna, I had several questions for her. First, why didn't she tell us of Cobb's threat to Odom? Second, was Lamia Odom getting additional money from Odom? Third, why was she climbing into Hogg's Rolls Royce that night?

And then there was Ted Odom. He had both opportunity and motive. From what I had learned, he stayed current with his bookies, so he wasn't faced with the prospect of coming up with unmanageable amounts of money.

And then the good father—Papa Poggy. He had reason, but unless Veronica Kinton was a much more accomplished liar than I thought, he had no opportunity.

Lamia Sue was dead, and I was left with Cobb, Maddox, Hogg, and Ted Odom.

At that moment, my cell rang. It was Casey the cab driver. When I questioned him about his fare the night of October second, he muttered, "Yeah, I think I remember."

I detected a devious note in his tone. "Think?"

"Yeah, but sometimes driving around, things get clearer."

With a chuckle, I asked. "How much driving around?"

"Oh," he drawled, "maybe twenty bucks' worth."

"Tell you what, Casey. Give me fifteen minutes, and I'll meet you out front of Grand Isle Inn."

"You got it."

Casey arrived ten minutes later. He hooked his thumb at the back door. "Hop in."

I opened the front door and offered his twenty bucks. "I'm not much in a mood for a drive. How's this?"

He arched an eyebrow and deftly pulled the bill from my fingers. His face lit in animation. "Yep, picked this dude up in front of that spooky old house at 8:40 or so. Dropped him off at the museum around nine."

"What did he look like?"

His face froze in a frown. He scratched his head. "Well, let's see . . ."

I handed him another twenty. A big smile played over his weathered face. "Slick looking. Like some college professor, you know, wearing one of them tweed coats with leather elbows. White hair smoothed back. A real high-class dude." He shrugged. "Suppose that's what he is. Going to that museum and all."

I grinned. Tweed jacket and leather elbows. Exactly what Maddox was wearing that night.

After Casey drove away, I headed for the garage—next stop, Ervin Maddox.

Chapter Twenty-four

If Ervin Maddox was surprised to see me, he hid it well. He arched an eyebrow and smiled. "Ah, Mr. Boudreaux. This is an unexpected pleasure." Dressed in a Polo shirt, running pants and shoes, he stepped back from the door. "Please excuse my dress. I wasn't expecting guests. Won't you come in?"

I stepped into the foyer. "I won't take long, Ervin."

He shook his head emphatically. "Take your time. I was watching the ballgame." He gestured to the den. "We can go in there."

"That isn't necessary. We can talk here."

A frown wrinkled his pale forehead. "If you wish."

Pulling out my note cards, I read aloud. "On October second, the Alamo Cab Company picked up a fare in front of the Wingate Museum of Art just after eight and took him to 2112 Fairchild. Around 8:40, the San

212

Antonio Cab Company picked up a fare at 2112 Fairchild and dropped him off at the museum at nine. The fare wore a tweed jacket with leather elbows." I glanced at Maddox whose face had frozen in alarm. "I know for a fact you left the lecture room at eight o'clock and did not return until around nine. The driver gave a description that is a perfect fit for you. I've no doubt when I show him your picture, he can identify you."

The frozen expression on his face slowly melted.

I continued. "I don't know if you've heard the news or not, but Lamia Sue Odom has been murdered. Although the justice of the peace declared Bernard Odom's death accidental, I believe Odom also was murdered. Now, you had motive."

Quickly, he tried to compose himself. "Motive? What motive?"

"Professional jealously for a start. You resented the fact that many in the art world considered Odom's professional accomplishments superior to yours. And you have a violent temper. With him out of the way, you were San Antonio's resident expert of antiquities."

He started to interrupt but I held up my hand. "I'm not one of those silvery-tongued prosecutors, but believe me, they can take that jealousy, couple it with the fact you had opportunity, and hand the grand jury a sound enough argument to put you on trial for felony murder."

I paused for a few seconds for my words to soak in. "Now, as far as I know, you might have left the lecture at five after eight and sat in the museum lobby until nine. All you have to do is come up with a reliable witness. Otherwise, your best bet is to tell the truth."

The slight man studied me a moment before dropping his gaze to the floor. He drew a deep breath, straightened his shoulders and smiled wanly. "If you don't mind, Mr. Boudreaux, I could use a drink."

In the den, he poured a straight Scotch, downed it, then poured another. He held up the glass to ask if I wanted one. I shook my head. He downed the second, then cleared his throat. "I was there that night. I was infuriated with Bernard regarding a recent authorship of an article in *National Archeology*, a scholarly publication most experts in the field of historical archeology consider the bible."

He hesitated when he saw the puzzled frown on my head. "Sometime back, Bernard suggested I join him at the Dallas County Museum of Natural History for joint research on the four miniature coffins containing the organs of Tutankhamen, who was born during the Eighteenth Dynasty. I—"

A red flag popped up in my head. "Hold on a minute. If I'm not mistaken, when I asked you before if you two had ever collaborated, you became indignant at the idea."

His pale face colored. In an almost inaudible voice, he muttered, "I'm sorry. I lied to you." He looked up at me hopefully. "When I learned he was dead, I was scared. I didn't want to be connected with him in any way at all."

I eyed the slight man warily. Tell one lie, and it's easy to tell a second. I nodded. "Go on."

"As I said, this was the first joint effort. The truth is, I thought maybe a relationship favorable to me might develop from our collaboration but I was mistaken. When the article was published, it bore his name only. I didn't know what I was going to do when I got to his house but I was furious. I planned to confront him at the exhibition in front of everyone but he didn't show up. So, I went to his house."

He paused, downed his drink, and poured a third. "We argued and got into a pushing match. I shoved him and he hit his head on the end table. I hurried to him, afraid I'd hurt him badly. But I hadn't. I helped him sit on the couch, and then he cursed me and shoved me away, telling me to get out." He paused and shrugged. "I did. He was sitting on the couch when I left."

"You say he hit his head."

Maddox nodded and touched a slender finger to his forehead. "Right here. It was bleeding a little."

"Not the back."

"No."

"And you say when you left, he was sitting on the couch?"

"Yes. He was bending over holding his forehead in his hands."

"Did anyone see you leave?"

"I don't know. The light was on in his secretary's office but I didn't see Edna."

"What time was that?"

"Around eight thirty or forty."

I jotted down my notes. "And Friday afternoon, say from noon to four, where were you?"

"Friday? This last Friday?"

"This last Friday."

He pondered the question a moment. "Oh, I spoke at the monthly meeting of the Daughters of the Alamo. It was an annual affair with members from around the state. It's held on the grounds behind the Alamo. I was there until after five."

I remembered the crowd I had spotted before I swung off the balcony of the Cattleman's.

Heading back toward the Odom mansion, I sorted my thoughts. I wanted to take a look at the den once again and see for myself just where Maddox left Odom on the couch. If Maddox was telling the truth, that meant that after he left, someone entered the den and saw Odom sitting on the couch, his head in his hands.

If someone had discovered him in that position, it would have been a simple matter to strike Odom on the back of his head, and then when he fell to the floor, suffocate him.

But why? The map or money or both?

Now, after the death of Lamia Sue, the only ones certain to benefit financially from Odom's death were Edna Hudson and Ted Odom.

Then there were Cobb, Hogg, and Maddox, all of whom would benefit from possession of the map.

A couple of discreet inquiries into the Daughters of

the Alamo and I would find out if Maddox had indeed been their speaker. That might absolve him from any connection with Lamia Sue's death but not Bernard Odom's.

In fact, I told myself, looking back over my notes, the only suspects not in the proximity of the Odom mansion that night were Papa Poggy and Lamia Sue, and she was dead.

The mansion was dark. No one answered the door.

Muttering a soft curse, I climbed in my Silverado and gave Joe Hogg a call, but his maid, Carmen, explained that he and his wife were attending the grand opening of a new dealership in Austin. "Mr. Hogg said they should be in late tonight. If not, first thing in the morning."

I thanked her and headed for the hotel, planning on going back over my notes and trying to find the pieces of Odom's puzzle that had escaped me.

And then, Jack Edney showed up.

Chapter Twenty-five

I had spent a couple of hours working on the last puzzle when there came a knock at the door. I hesitated, studying the puzzle for which I was desperately trying to find a key.

The knock came again.

I peered through the peephole and saw the pan-shaped face of Jack Edney wearing a worried expression. I rolled my eyes. The guy had impeccable timing. Every time I was in the middle of a job, he showed up.

Well, this time, I had some serious work to do if I wanted to have my facts straight for Chief Ibbara the next morning. I had no idea what was on his mind, but Jack would just have to go back to his little table on the River Walk where he could ogle the young ladies and guzzle his old fashioneds.

As soon as I opened the door, Jack rushed in, his eyes bright with excitement. "Tony, the cops got hold of me yesterday up in Austin."

I shrugged. "So? You told them what I said, didn't you?"

He nodded jerkily. "Word for word. That we just drove around San Antonio for an hour or so, then spent another hour or two on the River Walk, nowhere in particular. The cop tried to nail me down to a particular place but I told them I wasn't paying that much attention."

"Perfect." I grinned.

His frown deepened. "Yeah, but I don't think he bought it. He acted suspicious."

I laughed. "Cops and lawyers, by nature, are suspicious. They'll always think the worst." With a wry shrug, I added, "Unfortunately, they're right more often than not. But don't worry. That's exactly what we did, sightseeing around town and on the River Walk."

A tiny grin of relief crept onto his face. "I thought I did it right." He released a long sigh. "Well, I feel a little better now. For a while yesterday, I thought I was up to my neck in alligators, and they were chewing at you know what."

I laughed. "That bad, huh?"

His round face grew animated. "Tell me about it. I had to go back Friday night to handle a couple of problems at one of the complexes out on Highway

290. When I got up Saturday morning, all four tires were flat. Some joker had let the air out of them."

"And it isn't even Halloween yet."

Jack frowned. "It wasn't funny. And then the cop showed up. He stayed an hour or so. After he left, I was ready for a sugar fix, so I headed to Dooby's Donuts for some coffee and a couple of éclairs when I almost had a wreck. An idiot wrecker pulling one of those big pick-ups with the side all torn up pulled across the road right in front of me. I slid sideways trying to stop."

While I've never been a great believer in chance, I've knocked around this crazy world long enough to know that every so often, fortune steps up with a tanta-lizing offer impossible to believe. I started to laugh at his string of misfortunes but a niggling little thought tugged at me. "A big pickup?"

"Yeah. One of those with the big tires."

Suddenly, my pulse shifted into second gear. I was almost afraid to ask the next question. I had the feeling that several pieces of the puzzle might suddenly tum-ble into place if I got the right answer. "A red one?"

Jack frowned at me. "Yeah. Hey, how'd you know?"

My pulse hit third gear. "And it was the right side that was torn up?"

He nodded again. "Yeah. The passenger side."

"Where was the wrecker taking the pickup?"

His frown deepened. "Into some dealership."

"Which one?" I held my breath, waiting for that certain name.

Jack shrugged. "Beats me."

I muttered a curse under my breath and grabbed my jacket from the closet. "Where's your car?"

"In the parking lot. Why?"

I pulled him after me. "We're going for a ride."

As we headed up I-35, I brought Jack up to date since Friday. Ninety minutes after we left the hotel, we turned off I-35 onto Ben White Road. Two blocks down, Jack pointed to a car dealership. "There it is."

I looked in the direction he indicated. My hopes plummeted when I read the marquee in front of the dealership, COLEMAN AND SONS FORD.

Being a Sunday, the dealership was closed. I nodded to the locked gate. "Pull up there."

Jack braked the Cadillac to a gentle halt.

"Is this where the wrecker pulled in?"

"Yeah." Suddenly he stiffened and jabbed a finger toward the rear of the lot. "Hey! There's the pickup. At the back of the lot with those other wrecked cars."

Quickly I climbed from the car. "Wait here."

"Huh?" Jack frowned. "Where you going? The place is closed."

"I'll be right back," I said, swinging a leg over the locked gate. "Don't worry."

By now, the sun was dropping below the horizon, and from the clear sky, a blanket of chilly air settled over the city.

A sharp voice stopped me just before I reached the pickup. "Hey! What are you up to?"

I looked around as a uniformed security guard approached. "Hi."

An older man, he wore a frown. "The place is closed. You're trespassing."

"Sorry." I nodded to the pickup. "I was driving by and saw this off-roader. My son is out at UT. He has one like this, and I stay worried about him. You know how these kids are today with these things. They try to drive them over and through anything."

A knowing grin replaced the frown on his face. "Yeah, I know."

"Anyway, when I saw it, I almost had a heart attack. I just wanted to see if it was his. For all I know, he might have been hurt and ended up in the hospital, and I wasn't notified."

The older man shook his head. "Yeah. I got kids too. They're all growed up now but I still worry about them. Sure. I understand. I'd feel the same way. Go ahead and look."

"Thanks." I walked around the pickup, noting the deep scars on the passenger side of the pickup. The only identification was the dealer's license from Coleman and Sons Ford.

I grinned at him. "Nope. Not his. That's a relief." I headed back to the Cadillac.

"I'm glad," he said, falling in beside me.

Looking around at the expansive lot and buildings, I remarked, "This is some place here."

"Yeah. Ben Coleman owns it. Or he used to. Still owns a part of it."

I was too busy figuring out how to find the owner of the pickup to pay much attention to the older man. The only solution I could see was to make another trip over the next day, and then the word "Hogg" sliced through my concentration.

"What's that? Did you say Hogg?"

The security guard nodded. "Yep. Sure did. Old Ben was on the rocks, about to lose everything two years ago and Joe Hogg, who's got more car dealerships than the good Lord has angels, bailed him out for a share of the business." He paused and shrugged. "I don't know how much, but knowing that Hogg shyster, it was a big chunk."

I glanced around the lot. "I don't see any pickups here. Does Coleman have them on other lots?"

"Naw. He don't, but Hogg does." He gestured to the west. "He has them on a lot a few miles father down on Seventy-One."

"Some business." I whistled softly.

"Yep. Me, I don't care much for the man. Typical used car salesman, you know. Kinda greasy looking even, but to give the devil his due, he's done built hisself quite a business. Anything on four wheels, he sells."

We paused at the locked gate. I shook my head in awe. "You mean buses and eighteen-wheelers, big stuff like that?"

"Yep. Down in San Antone, I hear. He's always bidding on school buses and that sort of thing. Last I heard, the local school district there done bought over a hundred new buses last year."

I arched an eyebrow. "Not bad. Well, I appreciate you letting me take a look at that pickup. I feel a lot better now."

Jack shot me a quick glance as he pulled back into the traffic. "Was that it?"

I nodded slowly. "That was it. And somewhere in San Antonio, Hogg has a dealership that sells eighteen-wheeler tractors. That's our next stop."

"Fine with me, but let's grab something to eat on the way." Jack pulled into a Chubby's Barbecue where we picked up three sliced pork sandwiches. As we pulled away from the drive-thru, he hooked a thumb at the back seat. "Cold beer back there."

During the next hour and a half, I tried to rearrange my theories to take into account the new information I'd picked up.

If Hogg was behind the eighteen-wheeler and pickup, was he behind the other efforts to scare me off? If so, why? However I looked at his motives, they didn't make sense. Why would a successful businessman worth ten or so million risk it all for a map he planned to give to some university in exchange for a memorial to him? Unless there were reasons I had yet to discover.

Joe Hogg sold eighteen-wheelers from two dealerships, and I counted six black tractors on each lot, proving by themselves absolutely nothing.

So, now, all I had to do was figure out how to connect him with the tractor and the pickup that tried to run me off the road.

Jack dropped me off at the hotel and headed back to Austin.

Chapter Twenty-six

I awakened around four, my head filled with puzzles. Filling the courtesy coffeepot, I pulled out my notes and tackled the last puzzle once again.

For an hour and a half, I kept running into a brick wall, and then as I perused a fifteen-page booklet I'd downloaded on code breaking, I ran across an example of a ciphered code that had also been encrypted. The example was a transitional cipher used back during the Nixon administration in which the nineteen letters of the president's full name substituted for the first nineteen letters of the alphabet after which the remaining seven alphabetical characters were coded by A–F.

So, why couldn't the symbols be the encrypted code which, once matched with the appropriate key, divulged the message?

Remembering the number of times Odom had been referred to as an egocentric, I put in his name, Bernard Julius Odom, and ran down the alphabet to the letter P. Starting over with the remaining nine characters, I tagged them A-I.

The key, if it were the key, looked like this:

abcdefghijklmnopqrstuvwxyz
bernardjuliusodomabcdefghi

I glanced at my watch and muttered a curse. I jumped to my feet. I was running late. I'd finish the puzzle later but now I had to first bounce my murder theory off Chief Ibbara, if for nothing else to cover my behind; second, to replay the events of the night of October second in the Odom den as Ervin Maddox had laid them out; and third, to learn why Edna had said nothing of Leo Cobb's threat to Odom and to verify the Rolls she climbed into that night was Hogg's. In addition, I wanted to learn just how much of an allowance Lamia Sue received from her uncle. I knew what Ted had told me but I wanted to make sure. After all, she had been blackmailing Cobb. Who's to say she wasn't putting some kind of pressure on her uncle?

And then there was Joe Hogg. I had to wait on him. I had less than nothing to support my suspicions but perhaps I could gain some leverage from Edna Hudson. Of course, as far as I knew, that one night she climbed in his Rolls might have been the first time. I didn't think so but I would find out.

I had two pieces of business to take care of before I left for Ibbara's office. First, I called Jimmy Tamez, a local PI, and commissioned him to tail Joe Hogg. "If he picks up a woman at 2112 Fairchild in the evening, I want pictures, Jimmy. Clear ones. I've got to be able to ID her and the car."

"No sweat, Tony."

I stared at the receiver after I hung up. If that had been Edna climbing into Hogg's Rolls Royce, what was going on? Had he merely happened to be driving past and out of the goodness of his heart given her a lift? I doubted it. Was he fooling around on his show-girl wife with a fifty-two-year-old secretary? Not likely, but then, in my years on this planet, I'd learned the hard way never to say never.

Downstairs in the gift shop, I took care of my second piece of business. I purchased a small spray pump, half filled it with water, and dropped it in my pocket.

From behind the seat in my Silverado, I retrieved my bag of tools and rummaged through it, pulling out a vial of Luminol from a previous case. I dropped it in my pocket with the spray pump.

Chief Ibbara listened to my little theory, then promptly shot it down. "It could have happened that way, but I've got a justice of the peace who declared it an accidental death."

The lanky chief's reaction was what I had expected. Who could blame him? No sense in borrowing trouble, and that's exactly what the chief would be doing if he ignored the justice of the peace's ruling. "Just as long as you know, Chief. But, there is another factor involved that makes me think this is more than simply a missing map."

His bushy eyebrows knit. "Oh?"

"On the way down from Austin last Tuesday, an eighteen-wheeler ran me off the road."

A wry grin played over his swarthy face. "Welcome to Chicken Run," he said, referring to the name given that ninety-mile stretch of interstate from Austin to San Antonio because of the penchant of truckers to play chicken with smaller vehicles.

"There's more to it than that, Chief." I quickly detailed the incidents from the room tossing to the latest attempt at Devil's Backbone, with the exception of the setup with Lamia Sue Odom. When I finished, I paused. "I didn't mention it at first because I figured it was just another one of those incidents on the highway. But now I'm asking myself why."

He pursed his lips and gently stroked his mustache. "The map is worth a lot of money, right?"

"Yeah. That's what they say."

He smoothed his wavy hair. "I'm not telling you anything you don't know, but it's been my experience that people will pull a lot of crazy stunts for money."

He was right, of course, but I still felt there was more here than a mere theft. I changed the subject. "I heard about Lamia Sue Odom. A San Antonio detective questioned me. I'm sorry."

With a grimace, he muttered, "Sure hated that. She was my cousin. We weren't all that close but she was family. Her funeral's tomorrow." He paused and grew reflective. "She pulled a lot of stunts she shouldn't. But I'll give her credit. She didn't do it in my jurisdiction and put me on the spot."

I frowned, wondering if he meant what I thought he meant. "Are you talking about—"

"I'm not talking about anything."

When I saw the knowing look in his eye, I nodded. "I understand. Any leads?"

With a growl, he replied, "They won't say. There was enough drugs in her system to kill her but someone wanted to make certain and strangled her."

"Oh?" I remembered the red marks on her throat.

"Yeah. Small hands, the ME said."

"Small man or a woman, huh?"

"Yeah."

Just my luck, I told myself. Everyone on my list was five-eight or less.

Ibbara paused a moment, then leaned back in his chair and propped his feet on his desk. "Any closer to finding the map?"

"No." It was a lie but I figured the fewer who knew of what little success I'd gained the better. "Teddy gave me a list of possibles. Dead end on them." I paused. "It's still in that house somewhere. There's a couple of puzzles I'm trying to figure out. I think they are the solution." I had no sooner uttered the words than I wished I'd kept my mouth shut.

A frown knit his eyebrows. "Puzzles?"

I explained the two prints on the wall in the den.

A grin played over his swarthy face. "Hey, I'm not bad at puzzles. Why don't I go over there with you and see what you've got?"

I had wanted to be alone in the den so I could check for traces of blood, but I forced a laugh and pushed to my feet. "Come on. I won't turn down any help."

Wearing her usual one-piece print dress with her thin belt about her waist, Edna opened the door and smiled brightly, keeping her left hand at her side. "Louis, how good to see you." Her face crumpled into tears. "Wasn't it terrible about Lamia Sue?"

Ibbara put his arms around Edna and hugged. "Terrible. I know you'll miss her."

"We all will," she replied, backing away and brushing at the tears in her eyes. She smiled weakly at me. "Hello, Tony."

"Edna."

"Teddy isn't here."

Louis explained. "That isn't why we came over. We wanted to take a look at Uncle Bernard's office."

"Yeah," I said. "Chief Ibbara claims he's a whiz at puzzles. We'll soon see."

Edna accompanied us to the den. I pointed out the two puzzles on the wall. I didn't tell him of the work I had done on them. "There they are, Chief. So, what do you think?"

Print Number One

Π⊰⊱⊰⊱⊰⊱✳✛ ψ☺♌ξ⌂ℳ ⤳♈♒〰Ж♋⅋; ☯

Print Number Two

⊰〰β४〰〰Ⅱ ♋⌂Ⅱ〰♈⊱ ♌Ⅱ β⌂⊰♈〰

He whistled softly. "What makes you think those are puzzles? And what do they have to do with the map?"

"Leo Cobb—you know Leo?"

Ibbara nodded. "Yeah."

I paraphrased Cobb's remarks. "Cobb said that Odom once told him they were the solution to finding the map."

Ibbara frowned. "You couldn't prove it by me."

At that moment, the phone rang. Edna excused herself.

Ibbara moved closer to the prints. "What kind of figures are these?" He studied them a moment longer, and then with a shake of his head turned back to me. "You're a better man than me, Boudreaux, if you can figure them out."

I laughed. "I'm not much of a puzzle person. When I was a kid learning my catechisms, the sisters would sometimes administer tests in a crossword puzzle format. I flunked them all."

He shivered and stared at the palm of his hand. "Oh, yeah. The sisters. How well I remember them." He paused. "So, you got no idea?"

"No. There are so many different codes and ciphers, that unless a person has an idea of the key, they're almost impossible to solve."

He chuckled. "That sounds like Uncle Bernard." When I frowned, he gestured to the prints. "If those are puzzles, then he's probably grinning like a possum right now because no one could figure them out. He was like that. Biggest ego of anyone I've ever known." He arched an eyebrow. "Don't misunderstand, Boudreaux. I loved the old man, but if he hadn't been my kin, I would have probably detested him for the egomaniac he was."

At that moment, Edna reappeared. "Louis, it's the station. They need you."

"Be right there." He turned to me. "Hang in there, Boudreaux. You need anything, let me know."

I muttered a soft "Thank you, Lord," when Edna followed Louis from the den, closing the door behind her and leaving me alone. Quickly, I turned to the fabric couch next to the wall. According to Maddox, he helped Odom to the couch. When he left, Odom was sitting on the edge with his face buried in his hands.

Reconstructing the murder, I figured the killer entered from the door which was to the side of the couch, struck Odom on the back of his head, and when he discovered the old man was not dead, suffocated him with one of the throw pillows on the couch.

I glanced around the den, searching for the instrument the killer used to strike Odom. The lamps on the end tables were heavy brass, perfect for the job, but both had bulky shades, which would have made enough noise for Odom to look around.

No. The killer didn't use either lamp.

I scanned the den. Too bad Odom wasn't into medieval history. A mace or war ax would have been a juicy discovery.

Then my eyes settled on the two heavy gold crosses on either side of the door. I caught my breath. Was it possible?

My heart thudded against my chest as I inspected the crosses. A layer of dust covered the first, but on the second, the horizontal and vertical axis of the cross had been wiped clean. I looked closer, but there was no physical evidence visible to the eye. Quickly, I pulled out the spray pump in which I had poured a few ounces of water before I left the hotel, dumped in the vial of Luminol, and shook the pump vigorously.

Holding my breath the door wouldn't open, I quickly sprayed the cross, then drew the heavy drapes, plunging the room into gloom except for the dim bluish-green glow on the axis of the cross.

I was right. Bernard Odom had been murdered, and now I had one of the murder weapons.

Hastily, I sprayed the cushions from the couch. As the Luminol hit the second one, the same bluish-green glow appeared. Now I had both weapons.

Chapter Twenty-seven

Suppressing my excitement, I headed to Edna's office.

She was standing in front of the wall of pictures, straightening them. She smiled warmly. "Any luck, Tony?"

I said nothing about what little progress I'd made. I shrugged. "To tell the truth, I'm getting nowhere."

Edna frowned in disappointment. "I'm sorry. You've looked everywhere in the den?" She straightened a picture on the wall and stepped back to study it.

"Yeah. Everywhere." I sighed. "Shame about Lamia Sue. Have you heard anything about her?"

"No. The funeral's tomorrow at two. Teddy wanted it here at the house, and then we'll take her to the mausoleum. You're more than welcome." She indicated the picture. "Here's one of her last year."

I studied the picture. It was Lamia Sue and Edna on the porch. "She was a pretty little thing," I whispered.

Beside the picture was the one of Edna at The Clock I had seen earlier. She was seated on a bench in front of the translucent clock with her silver watch glistening on her left wrist while her hand carefully covered the other in her lap. Like the first time I looked at it, something seemed out of place. I glanced at the one of her and Lamia Sue, trying to discern the difference, but with no luck.

I studied the older woman for a few moments. Her eyes reflected the anguish she was feeling. "Sorry."

She drew a deep breath. "It's a sad thing but something like that was inevitable for her."

"Because of her drugs?"

Edna looked at me in surprise. "You knew?"

"Yeah. I learned she was a stringer."

"Stringer?"

"Sold drugs for a dealer."

"Oh. I didn't know that."

"It's a shame. Here she was, a pretty young woman with a nice income from her uncle. And then this happens."

A sad smile played over Edna's thin lips.

I played dumb. "What kind of allowance did Odom provide for her? A couple thousand a month?"

Edna's eyes grew wide and a tiny smile curled her lips. "Two thousand? Heavens no."

I frowned. "Oh? Not that much, huh?"

She shook her head emphatically. "Oh, no. Much more. Eight thousand."

"Eight thous—" I whistled softly. The figure surprised me, but not for the reason she thought. "Eight thousand?"

"Yes. Mr. Odom could afford it. He was a very generous man."

"He must have been." I couldn't help wondering if Ted knew how much his father had been giving his cousin. And then I began to question whether or not Teddy had given me the correct figure on his allowance. "Teddy told me that his allowance was five thousand a month. Is that about right?"

Edna shifted about in her chair. "Yes."

I frowned. "Why the difference?"

She shrugged. "That was Mr. Odom. He was always harder on Teddy than Lamia Sue. He was always much more protective of her than of Teddy."

"Does Teddy know?" I knew the answer but I was curious as to her response.

Slowly she shook her head. "Mr. Odom instructed me to keep it quiet. Teddy never asked."

"Lamia Sue didn't tell him?"

"No. She knew to keep it quiet also."

At that moment, I felt a sense of genuine sorrow for Teddy Odom and a sense of growing dislike for his old man.

Edna sensed my irritation. She hurried to explain. "Mr. Odom would have done anything in the world for Teddy or Lamia Sue. He was truly a good man. He just wanted his son to stand on his own two feet."

I drew a deep breath. "I can understand that." I

changed the subject. "By the way. You might have mentioned it earlier, and I just forgot, or it went in one ear and out the other."

"Oh? What was that?"

"Well, when I was interviewing Leo Cobb, he admitted he had threatened to kill Odom in front of you, but I don't remember you mentioning that."

For a fleeting moment, she froze, her dark eyes growing hard, but in the next instant they softened. She gave me a tolerant smile. "Leo and Mr. Odom were friends for years. He didn't mean what he said, and I couldn't see any reason to stir up trouble for him." She shrugged. "He's got enough problems as it is."

Not wanting her to sense my skepticism at her reply, I laughed. "I know what you mean. Oh, and one other question. A few days ago, Rebecca Wentworth told me Mr. Odom had mentioned donating the Piri Reis to the Wingate Museum of Art. Did he ever say anything to you about it?"

She laughed softly and waved the idea aside. "Nothing to it. Oh, he did mention it once, but decided not to."

"Did he say why?"

"No. I'm sorry."

I started to ask her about the Rolls and Joe Hogg, but decided to wait.

As I drove away from the mansion, I was ticking off the tasks that lay ahead. First, being away from the puzzle had cleared my head. I was anxious to return and see if my newest idea was the key.

Then, I wanted to check the bank accounts Eddie Dyson had provided to find out just what kind of allowance the old man gave the kids.

I picked up a soft drink in the lobby of the hotel. Upstairs, I popped it open and glanced idly at the financial information Eddie had sent.

Regular deposits of five thousand a month were made to both Lamia Sue and Teddy's bank accounts. I frowned. Teddy's made sense, but where was the other three thousand that Edna said the young woman had been receiving?

Glancing at Edna's account, I saw she had an automatic deposit of forty-eight hundred a month. Her balance was a little over ten Gs and her savings were close to thirty. I suspected she had a few annuities or 401, which was certainly not unusual for a single woman on the same job for over thirty years. Thirty-four to be exact.

I stared out over the balcony at the River Walk below, sipping my water and wondering about the other three thousand Lamia Sue was supposed to be getting.

Dusk crept over the city. Bright lights began punching gay holes in the growing darkness. Below, several young women in jeans and scanty blouses strolled the River Walk, giggling and hugging their bare arms against the sudden chill. On impulse, I grabbed my jacket and headed for the Elena Towers wondering if Lamia Sue's so-called roommate was around.

* * *

The clerk at the front desk of the Elena Towers solemnly informed me that Lamia Sue Odom had suddenly passed away. Feigning surprise, I frowned and shook my head at the young woman. "That's too bad. Does she have any family around that you know of?" Before she could reply, I patted my coat pocket and continued. "I was hired to give her an important document that is very valuable. I have no idea what it is, but the attorney told me it was worth several thousand dollars to her. So, you can see my predicament."

The brown-haired clerk pursed her lips. "I'm sorry. I don't know, but maybe her roommate would be able to help."

"That would be ideal. Can I see him?"

She smiled awkwardly. "It's a her, but she's out right now."

I gave her my room and telephone number at the Grand Isle. "I'll be there all evening. And there is a finder's fee for helping us contact the appropriate individuals."

Back in my room, I pulled out the second puzzle along with the partial translation I had come up with earlier.

Print Number Two

⚯⚯⚯⚯⚯⚯Ⅱ ⚯⚯Ⅱ⚯⚯⚯ ⚯Ⅱ ⚯⚯⚯⚯⚯

EH_HH_ __D_H _ __ _DE_H

Assuming the spacing in the puzzle indicated four words, I saw I was missing two characters in the first, four in the second, all in the third, and two in the fourth.

I pulled out the new key and tried to fit the puzzle into it.

abcdefghijklmnopqrstuvwxyz
bernardjuliusodomabcdefghi

The encrypted code was simple to apply. The first character in the translation was an E, and the E in Bernard transposed to a B in the alphabet.

Quickly I transposed the others, coming up with BY YY in the first word, GY in the second, and in the fourth, GB Y.

<u>BY</u> <u>YY</u> <u>GY</u> <u>GB</u> Y

Nothing! Pure gibberish.

Could it be Bernard Odom was playing one big joke on everyone? No. I couldn't believe it. The map did exist. I squeezed my eyes shut in frustration. The map did exist, but what did that crazy old man do with it?

A knock at the door caused me to jump.

I glanced at my watch, surprised to see it was almost nine o'clock. I peered through the viewer. My frustration vanished. It was the same young woman I had seen with Lamia Sue outside the Elena Towers last week.

Chapter Twenty-eight

I opened the door. "Yes?"

The hollow-eyed woman glanced up and down the hall warily. "You the guy looking for Lamia Sue?"

"Oh? Are you her roommate?"

"Yeah. She's dead, you know."

I stepped back. "I know. Won't you come in?" She hesitated. I stepped back in the room. "We'll leave the door open, okay?"

I moved across the room and sat on the couch next to the outside wall. She followed me in, pausing just before she reached the bed. Her eyes took in the room with an animal wariness, and she fiddled absently with a missing button on her blouse. Her wristwatch slid down her thin wrist.

At that moment, I knew what had struck me as odd

about the photograph in Edna's office of her at the The Clock the night she went to Don Quick's concert. In the snapshot, her watch was on her left hand, not the right.

The young woman cleared her throat. "The clerk said you had something for her family?"

"And a nice fee for whoever helps me."

She dragged the tip of her tongue across her dry lips. "So what is it?"

"Your fee?" I pointed to a sealed envelope on the end table by the couch. "Five hundred bucks. Interested?"

Her eyes lit with greed. "Maybe."

I leaned back on the couch. "Look, I'm really after information, and it's worth five big ones. Still interested?"

She hesitated, eyeing me warily. "I didn't have nothing to do with her death."

"That's not why I'm here. You won't be involved in a thing. In fact, I don't even want to know your name."

Her eyes studied me for several moments and then she nodded. "Name's Leslie. What do you want to know?"

"Were you with her long?"

"Ever since she got back in town about six months ago."

"Look, I know she was a stringer." Her eyes grew wide. I quickly reassured her. "This isn't about the drugs. You know she received a monthly allowance from her uncle, didn't you?"

"Sure. That was no secret."

I drew a deep breath. "I heard it was close to ten thousand a month."

The wary tension on her gaunt face broke into a wreath of smiles. "Ten thousand. I wish. Someone's been feeding you a line, friend. Five thousand from the old man. She picked up another three thousand in cash, but I don't know where it come from for sure."

"Cash?" I frowned, remembering Cobb's monthly payoff, which was two thousand. Was Lamia Sue blackmailing someone else? I didn't have to pretend I was puzzled, for I was. Edna claimed Odom gave Lamia Sue eight thousand. Someone was lying or else my young friend didn't know what she was talking about. "Are you sure, Leslie? I would have sworn they told me ten."

Relaxing some, she replied, "I've seen the checks when she deposited them. All signed by her uncle."

I studied her another moment. "That three thousand in cash. Was it from the dealing?"

She shook her head emphatically. "No, that was extra."

"Any idea where she got it?"

Leslie eyed me for several moments. "Once I was with her when a small, fat little man handed her an envelope down on the River Walk. There was cash in it. I guess maybe from him."

Cobb flashed to mind. Had he lied to me? Was he dishing out three thousand a month to her? Why would he lie over another thousand? I picked up the envelope and tossed it on the bed in front of her. "There you are. Paid in full."

She eyed me suspiciously, then grabbed the envelope and stuffed it in her pocket.

"Are you going to count it?"

A sly smile curled her lips. "It's there." She turned to the door, then hesitated and looked back at me.

"You a cop?"

"PI."

"You know anything about her death?"

"Only that she was strangled. Do you?"

She pressed her lips together. "Not about that, but I was with her when she got a call to go down to the hotel."

I tried to still my excitement. "She say who it was from?"

"No, but the way she talked, she expected a larger check in the months to come."

"Are you sure?"

She arched an eyebrow. "I'm sure."

I sat staring at the open door for several minutes after she left. If Lamia Sue expected a larger check, then she was trying to up the ante on someone, but who?

While the young woman's brain cells were probably down to the last few hundred, Leslie seemed certain about the five thousand dollar allowance. Still, I reminded myself, her answers could be nothing more than a residual carryover from the drugs she poked up her nostrils.

Still, it was something to consider.

My stomach growled. I'd forgotten all about dinner

but I was too tired to go out. After a shower, I climbed into bed and finally dropped off into a troubled sleep.

Rising early next morning, I popped down to the lobby for coffee and a couple of bagels from the inn's continental breakfast buffet.

Back in my room, I glanced at the unsolved puzzle. I was fresh out of ideas, so instead, while nibbling on the bagels, I turned back to the information from the night before. According to the young woman, Lamia's allowance was five thousand. Edna claimed it was eight.

And then Lamia was called to the hotel in anticipation of receiving more money. Instead, she was murdered. By the same perp who murdered Bernard Odom. Had I not checked Cobb's whereabouts, I would have figured he was the one but he had a solid alibi.

I leaned back and stared at the pile of note cards, a sinking feeling beginning to grow in my stomach. She couldn't have been blackmailing her uncle. Edna would have known, for she wrote out the checks. And what about the other three thousand a month? Leslie claimed she had seen some of the checks. If Lamia Sue was getting the three thousand, where was it going?

Pulling out my note cards, I spread them over the table.

Starting back at the beginning, I tried to reconstruct that night. Odom was in his den. After telling him good night, Edna left at her regular time. She saw a white car outside, Joe Hogg's, but he claimed he didn't drive up until 7:45, then departed without going inside. Why would he lie about that? At eight Ted returned Odom's encyclopedia of ancient maps to his uncle. Then around 8:20 Maddox arrived. He and Odom argued, and he shoved Odom to the floor. When Cobb arrived at nine thirty Odom was dead, suffocated. At eleven o'clock, Ted Odom discovered his father's body.

I studied the time line. I was missing something, but what?

At that moment, the phone rang. I glanced at my watch. Just after ten. It was Jimmy Tamez. "Got your stuff, Tony."

"Great. Was it what I thought?'

"Not exactly."

I grimaced.

"The woman caught a cab when she left work. I got a good shot of her. On a hunch, I followed the cab. She got out at the corner of Fannin and Sepulta and climbed into a gray Rolls Royce. I ran the tag."

"Don't tell me. Joe Hogg."

"Exactly. I'm sending the shots over to you now."

After hanging up, I went back over my note cards, rearranging them to put a different perspective on the case.

I went back and reread the scenario I had just recreated of the night of Odom's death. Halfway through, I caught my breath. Hastily, I thumbed through my cards, pulling out one of the first ones I had jotted down when I interviewed Edna.

*"Yes. I came up here that night, and he was sit-
ting at his desk reading one of his favorite books,
the* Dictionary of Ancient Phoenician Maps.*"*

Fumbling through my cards, I found the one detail-
ing my interview with Joe Hogg.

*"Yeah, I got there about seven forty-five or so, but
I didn't go in the house. I went there to make a final offer on the map. I sat in the car a moment,
then decided not to. I drove away."*

I leaned back and stared at the cards on the table before me. After a few moments collecting my thoughts, I
called Chief Ibbara. He was out and wouldn't be back
until after the funeral.

Just before I left for the funeral, Tamez's photos arrived. They were perfect.

Chapter Twenty-nine

Only a select handful of mourners attended Lamia Sue's funeral at two o'clock that afternoon. I sat at the rear of the room, trying to be as unobtrusive as possible.

After the service, Chief Ibbara and I remained behind as the small contingent passed in front of us and climbed into the limousine behind the hearse. I paid particular attention to Edna. Her watch was on her right wrist.

After the small procession of vehicles disappeared around the corner, Ibbara glanced at me. "So, what's up?"

Keeping my suspicions to myself, I headed back in the house, explaining I'd turned up some puzzling questions about Bernard Odom's finances for the last few years. I wanted a court order to open the records.

Ibbara jerked to a halt before entering Edna's office. "You're nuts. Why?"

I studied the snapshot of Edna at The Clock. Her watch was on her left wrist, and it was her left hand covering the right. There was no brown patch on her left hand. My eyes moved up to her dress. It buttoned like a man's, from the right. My heart thudded against my chest. Struggling to control my excitement, I muttered, "Just say I got an idea. So how about humoring me? Can you get them?" I looked around at him, keeping my suspicions to myself.

He shook his head emphatically. "Ain't no way. You know I can't get a judge to authorize something like that just because I want them. I got no probable cause. Can you get that for me?"

I glanced at the old watchtower three stories above us, remembering the years of files stored there. "Maybe." I paused, then nodded. "Yeah, I think I—"

"I don't want to know nothing. Just get it."

After Ibbara left, I called Leo Cobb. He reaffirmed that his blackmail money was only two thousand a month. I headed for Joe Hogg's. While I didn't have hard evidence, I figured I had enough to make him wonder. And maybe that would lead me to some. And maybe it wouldn't.

Hogg answered the door himself. With a genial smile, he invited me in. "Still looking for that map, huh?" He gestured to a chair at the patio table. "What's your poison?" he asked, opening up a portable bar in the shade of the awning.

While he appeared amiable enough, I sensed an undercurrent of uneasiness. "Anything cold."

He mixed us a couple of icy rum Collins, heavy on the rum, easy on the Collins. He plopped heavily into a wrought-iron chair that I expected to bend with his bulk. It didn't, but it groaned. "So, what can I do for you today?"

I sipped my drink and looked him straight in the eyes. "First, tell me once again about where you were on October second."

He pressed his lips together tightly. "I told you once."

"I know but tell me again."

After a drawn-out sigh, he repeated his story, the same one he had told earlier.

"And you're certain it was seven forty-five?"

"Yeah. I told you before. And then I went down to the Alamo Sports Bar. Like I told you before, you can ask Ca—"

"I know, I know. Calvin. Now, one more thing. What's going on between you and Edna Hudson?"

His bottom jaw hit the table. He sputtered. Sweat popped out on his forehead.

Before he could mutter anything intelligible, I tossed the photos on the table. "Maybe these will refresh your memory."

Like a deflating balloon, his belligerence collapsed. Numbly, he stared at them. He glanced at me, his dark eyes studying me with an animal wariness. "I'm not fooling around on my wife, if that's what you got in mind."

"I don't know what I've got in mind, Joe. You tell me."

He licked his lips. "Look, Edna and me, we're just friends. We go way back. Edna, she's unmarried. Truth is, I always felt kinda sorry for her. Odom was a pompous jerk. He treated her like dirt. It's a lonesome life she's got; no family, no kids. Sometimes we just go out for kicks. That's all there is to it."

He was lying. I could see it in his eyes. "The cops might have a different idea."

A faint smile curled his lips. "Fine with me. I got nothing to hide. I didn't have nothing to do with the map. I got no idea where it is."

I wanted to confront him about the off-roader and the eighteen-wheel tractor, but I knew all he had to do was deny any involvement and I couldn't prove otherwise. I tried a different angle. "For your information, Joe, someone murdered Lamia Sue Odom."

He stared at me in disbelief. "What?" He swallowed hard. "But, I thought she'd ODed. That's what the news said."

"She had enough in her system to kill her, but someone made sure. They strangled her. From what I hear, the forensics guys say the killer was a man with small hands." I glanced at the smaller man's hands. "About like yours."

During the afternoon, a cold front blasted in, driving the temperatures down to near freezing. I couldn't help thinking what a lousy day it had been for a funeral. I eyed the leaden clouds overhead. A gloomy day, and the night promised to be even more dismal.

Dropping by the hotel, I picked up the puzzle and headed back to the mansion, parking a couple of blocks away. I didn't know what time Ted and Edna returned from the mausoleum or if they did. I would just have to wait and see. While I waited, I worked on the puzzle with the same lack of success as earlier.

Edna left promptly at seven o'clock, catching her cab and disappearing into the night. A few minutes later, Ted left, leaving the old mansion in darkness.

Folding the puzzle into my pocket, I waited another fifteen minutes, then ghosted through the darkness to the basement door beneath the rear delivery ramp. The icy wind cut through my jacket. I quickly picked the lock. Using a tiny penlight, I made my way up the spiral stairway to the storage room in the watchtower on the third floor.

I figured Edna's books for the last five or six years were on her computer, and I didn't have her password. But there were always the records in journals and ledgers upstairs in the file cabinets.

I'll say this for Edna, every cabinet was marked clearly. I opened the 2001 cabinet and pulled out a thick ledger.

Staying away from the windows, I knelt on the floor and a big grin spread over my face as I thumbed through the 2001 expense ledger. There was a great deal of activity, but I noted that each month a five thousand dollar payment went to both Lamia Sue and Ted Odom. At the same time, I noticed a two thousand dollar check made out to Tabors Family Health Center and another check, this one a thousand, to FC Motors for vehicular maintenance.

A creak sounded from the darkness. I cut off my penlight and remained motionless. The cold darkness seeped into my bones, and the ancient house creaked and groaned as the wind buffeted it.

After several minutes of silence, I snapped on the penlight and thumbed back through previous ledgers where I discovered Odom had been a regular benefactor for the last ten years to the Tabors Family Health Center. The monthly check to the motor company began in 2001.

But nowhere I looked could I find evidence of Lamia Sue receiving eight thousand a month from her uncle. Now, I told myself, staring off into the darkness surrounding me, if I were suspicious like Al Grogan, I'd figure that the two Gs to the family center and the other G to the motor company were part of the eight.

If that were true, there was only one explanation. I shook my head in disbelief, wondering just how long Edna Hudson had been embezzling funds from the old man. In that flash of understanding, I realized Lamia Sue must have somehow discovered Edna's embezzling and was blackmailing her for a thousand a month of hush money. That thousand with Cobb's made the three thousand.

And just as suddenly, I knew who had murdered Bernard Odom.

There was only one with opportunity and motive—Edna Hudson.

I sat staring into the darkness. She had lied from the beginning. I knew now what had been bothering me about the time line of that night. She could not have left at seven. She didn't see Hogg's Cadillac until seven forty-five.

Sometimes a sudden epiphany of recognition opens other links in a case. I suddenly realized that Edna had no way of knowing Odom was studying the encyclopedia of ancient maps when she stopped in his office, for Ted hadn't returned the encyclopedia until eight o'clock, an hour after she was supposed to have left. And then according to Maddox, the light was on in her office at eight thirty, which meant she was there. My heart thudded in my chest, and my pulse raced. "Jeez," I muttered, pushing to my feet and sliding the ledger under my arm. I had to get to Chief Ibbara.

Holding the tiny beam to the floor to prevent any peripheral light to show in the windows, I headed for the stairs.

No sooner had I stepped out of the watchtower than my head exploded, and I felt myself falling into a deep, black hole.

Chapter Thirty

The next thing I remembered were voices some-where far off in the darkness, vague sounds drifting through the muddled confusion in my head. "Have you lost your mind? You might have killed the guy." The husky voice was familiar, but in my numbed state I didn't recognize it.

I tried to move but my arms were tied behind me.

A woman's voice I recognized as Edna's broke in. "Hush. Help me get him down to the car before Teddy gets back."

Rough hands jerked me to my feet. My head spun as I stumbled down the stairs, half-falling, half-staggering. I stumbled and fell when we reached the first floor.

The man's voice spoke again. This time I recognized it as Joe Hogg's. "Wait a minute, Edna. I asked you. What are you going to do with him?"

Her voice was urgent. "What do you think? We don't have a choice. Get him up."

He protested. "You mean, *you* don't have a choice. I don't mind helping you steal the map but even if you are my sister I'm not going to be a party to killing anyone."

Sister! His words cleared the fog in my brain instantly. Because of Ted's anticipated appearance at any moment, I didn't figure she would take a chance on killing me in the mansion. I managed to croak out, "You're already part of it, Hogg. She suffocated the old man."

Hogg jerked around. "What's that?"

In the dim glow of the flashlight, I saw the fear on Edna's face. "Don't listen to him. I wasn't even here when Mr. Odom had his accident. I was at a concert."

Despite the throbbing in my head, I tried to form my words carefully. "Don't listen to her, Hogg. She's smart. The Clock was a slick alibi. I got to hand it to you, Edna. Get a picture at ten minutes after three, and then reverse it on your computer so it shows ten until nine, ten minutes before his death."

"You're crazy."

"No. I would never have caught that except your dress was buttoned on the wrong side and your left hand was covering your right."

Hogg looked around at her. "Edna? What's he talking about?"

"And ask her about Lamia Sue Odom."

"Don't listen to him, Joe. I told you I had nothing to do with her death."

"She's lying, Hogg. Lamia Sue was blackmailing her because she found out your sister was embezzling two thousand a month from the old man. I don't know for how many years, but I checked back fifteen and she was doing it then."

"Liar!" she screamed, kicking me in the side of the head.

Stars exploded in my skull. Somewhere, I could hear the two of them arguing. I don't know how long they screamed at each other but finally Edna grew calm. "Listen to me, Joe. It was all an accident. When I went up to the den he was bleeding. I tried to help him but he went crazy. He cursed me and slapped me. I pushed him away and he fell on the couch. I grabbed the first thing I could find and hit him before he could get up." She paused. "He was unconscious but still alive. I panicked and smothered him so he couldn't tell anyone. Lamia Sue walked in. She threatened to go to the police if I didn't double her allowance. The map is still in the house. I need time to find it. If we don't get rid of Boudreaux, then it's all over."

Running my tongue over my dry lips, I forced a laugh. "You'll never find it but I know where it is."

"What?" Edna said.

Hogg stammered. "You—you think he really does?"

"He's lying," she hissed through clenched teeth. "Let's get him out of here."

I grunted. "Maybe not."

A bright light flashed in my eyes, blinding me. Edna stuck her face in front of mine. "Where is it?"

Shaking my head to clear the webs, I realized I was operating on borrowed time. I didn't figure Hogg was strong enough to stop his sister from whatever she had in mind, so if I was going to get out of this mess I had to do it myself.

"In the den," I muttered, struggling to collect my thoughts. I twisted my wrists, discovering they were bound with some type of cloth.

"Impossible. I've torn the den apart."

I snorted. "Not enough."

They jerked me to my feet and shoved me across the floor to the den. "Then show us, smart man," she said, jamming the muzzle of what felt like an automatic in my back.

Hogg opened the door and flipped on the light. Edna shoved me into one of the wingback chairs. "All right. Now where is it?"

I nodded to the bookcase. "Up there. Behind the top shelf."

Her eyes narrowed. "How do you know that?" She eyed me suspiciously.

"I know."

"You're lying."

"Then forget it."

Without taking her eyes off me, she said, "Take a look, Joe."

He groaned as he stood on a chair and stretched for the top shelf. "I can't reach it."

Edna muttered. "Come here and watch him. I'll do it myself." She handed him the automatic and climbed up on the chair and began tossing books to the floor.

I looked up at Hogg, at the same time flexing my wrists to loosen my bonds. Under my breath, I muttered, "You better get while you can, Joe. She lied to you about the old man and Lamia Sue. You're not part of this, yet." That was a lie also, but one that I felt was well justified.

The cloth around my wrists was beginning to give.

Joe kept turning his eyes to her, and whenever he did I worked my wrists. If I could get the jump on him while she was still on the chair I had a chance. Without warning, my hands popped free.

Suddenly, she screamed. She had leaned too far to one side, and the chair began to topple.

Joe looked around momentarily. I leaped at him, sending the automatic sliding across the room.

Edna hit the floor. For a moment, she didn't move, and then she rolled over, the automatic in hand, and the muzzle pointed straight at my belly.

At that moment the den door opened and Ted stepped in. The grin on his face vanished when he saw Edna holding the automatic. His eyes darted to Hogg. "Hey, what's going on here? Edna—"

With a scream of rage, she jerked around and fired.

I leaped behind the couch as half a dozen shots rang out. I heard the door of the den slam and then the front door. Moments later, a terrified scream cut through the silence.

When I looked up, Ted was sprawled on the floor,

and Hogg was slumped on the couch. I hurried to Ted. He had a bloody shoulder but that was his only wound. He tried to speak. "What—what—"

I jammed a handkerchief over his shoulder and pressed his hand to it. "I'll explain later." I glanced at Hogg who was moaning and cradling his belly in his arms. I jumped to my feet and raced after Edna.

From the front door all I saw was darkness. I jerked to a halt on the porch and stared at the sidewalk below. I flipped on the porchlights.

A dark figure lay sprawled on the concrete. Edna! Even from this distance, I could see her head was twisted at a grotesque angle.

Chapter Thirty-one

Chief Ibbara glanced around the den. "Who would have believed it? Edna had been with Uncle Bernard thirty-four years."

Ted, his arm in a sling, muttered, "I can't figure it. She was like a sister to me." He frowned at me. "What made her do it?"

All I could do was shrug. "Well, from all I learned, your father wasn't an easy man to get along with."

Ibbara laughed. "No offense, Teddy, but I don't see how she lasted all that time with your father."

Teddy grinned ruefully. "No offense taken. He had a temper. I didn't like being around him, but at least I could get out of here when I wanted." He shook his head. "She couldn't. In a way, I feel sorry for her."

"Yeah," Ibbara replied. "And after all that still no

262

map." He grinned at me. "What made you first suspect her?"

I tried to smile, but the side of my face was swollen from Edna's well-delivered kick. "I almost didn't. I guess I started wondering when I saw the picture of her with her wristwatch on her left wrist. I—" A wild idea suddenly popped into my head.

Hastily, I fumbled for the puzzle in my pocket. I spread it on the large table.

"That's Father's puzzle."

I glanced at Teddy. "Yeah. Now take a look."

⮡ᨊᚼᨊᨊ∏ ᚼ⚍∏ᨊᚼᩞ ᔐ∏ ᚼ⚍⮡ᩞᨊ

EH_HH_D_H_ _ _DE_H

"The characters at the bottom are the only ones I could decipher. They're characters in various fonts but they make no sense. You see, Edna used her computer to flip-flop her picture at The Clock, making her right hand appear as her left. What if your father did the same thing, more or less, sort of flip-flopped, substituted one character for the other?"

Ibbara frowned. "You mean, like that E means another letter?"

I nodded. "Look at all the Hs. Five of them. Since E is the most frequent letter in our alphabet, let's give that value to H."

I wrote out the alphabet. ABCDEFGHIJKLMNOPQ

RSTUVWXYZ. "Take a look. H is three letters removed from E. Let's try that." Quickly, we transposed the characters. E became a B, H an E, and D an A.

EH HH	*D H*	_	*DE H*
BE EE	*A E*		*AB E*

Ted pointed to the third word. "That one has two letters. Could they been an IN?"

Ibbara grunted. "The first character sort of looks like a capital I, huh?"

"Yeah," said Ted. "And that roman numeral two would be the N."

Excited, I replied, "Look. There's three of those twos."

Our next translation came up as BE__EEN_ANE__ IN _AB_E.

"The first word has to be 'between,' " said the chief. "And that curlicue-looking character that's a T is on the last word. That makes it TAB_E."

"Table!" Ted shouted, stepping back and staring down at the table on which we had spread the puzzle. "And look, there's another L in the second word, _ANEL."

"Panel. Or panels," I said, glancing under the table. I read the translation. "BETWEEN PANELS IN TABLE."

Ibbara pointed to dark panels at either end of the table on which a lion's head rose in relief.

Five minutes later, with the aid of a screwdriver, Ibbara removed the back of one panel. "Well, I'll be," he muttered, his voice muffled. With a grunt, he slid from under the table a well-worn leather portfolio. He handed it to Teddy, who fumbled to open it.